P9-CFA-458

The
Sweet
revenge
of
Celia
Door

The Sweet revenge of Celia Door

karen finneyfrock

Viking

An imprint of Penguin Group (USA) Inc.

VIKING

Published by the Penguin Group

Penguin Group (USA) Inc., 345 Hudson Street, New York, New York 10014, U.S.A.

Penguin Group (Canada), 90 Eglinton Avenue East, Suite 700, Toronto, Ontario, Canada M4P
2Y3 (a division of Pearson Penguin Canada Inc.)

Penguin Books Ltd, 80 Strand, London WC2R 0RL, England

Penguin Ireland, 25 St Stephen's Green, Dublin 2, Ireland (a division of Penguin Books Ltd)

Penguin Group (Australia), 250 Camberwell Road, Camberwell, Victoria 3124, Australia (a
division of Pearson Australia Group Pty Ltd)

Penguin Books India Pvt Ltd, 11 Community Centre, Panchsheel Park, New Delhi – 110 017, India

Penguin Group (NZ), 67 Apollo Drive, Rosedale, Auckland 0632, New Zealand
(a division of Pearson New Zealand Ltd.)

Penguin Books (South Africa) (Pty) Ltd, 24 Sturdee Avenue, Rosebank,
Johannesburg 2196, South Africa

Penguin Books Ltd, Registered Offices: 80 Strand, London WC2R 0RL, England

First published in the United States of America by Viking,
an imprint of Penguin Group (USA) Inc., 2013

1   3   5   7   9   10   8   6   4   2

LIBRARY OF CONGRESS CATALOGING-IN-PUBLICATION DATA
Finneyfrock, Karen.
The sweet revenge of Celia Door / by Karen Finneyfrock.
p. cm.
Summary: Fourteen-year-old Celia, hurt by her parents' separation, the loss of her only friend,
and a classmate's cruelty, has only her poetry for solace until newcomer Drake Berlin befriends her,
comes out to her, and seeks her help in connecting with the boy he left behind.
ISBN 978-0-670-01275-6 (hardcover)
[1. High schools—Fiction. 2. Schools—Fiction. 3. Revenge—Fiction. 4. Gays—Fiction.
5. Poetry—Fiction. 6. Family life—Pennsylvania—Hershey—Fiction.
7. Hershey (Pa.)—Fiction.] I. Title.
PZ7.F49835Swe 2013   [Fic]—dc23   2011047221

Printed in U.S.A.   Set in Berling LT   Book design by Nancy Brennan

ALWAYS LEARNING   PEARSON

For Molly Eleanor Rhoades

✗　✗　✗

The Sweet revenge of Celia Door

CHAPTER

I

At fourteen I turned Dark. Now I'm Celia the Dark.

The first day of ninth grade, I walked twenty blocks from my house to Hershey High School in boots so thick, it looked like I grew three inches over the summer. I wore a gray shirt under a black hoodie, which was pulled down so far over my forehead, it met my eyeliner. I swept in through the side entrance, located my locker on the second floor, and used masking tape to hang a sign on the door. It was made of black cardboard and letters cut out of magazines like a ransom note.

Some kids, I've been told, come to school to learn. Some come for the social outlet or because they love theatre or football. Most come because it is legally required by the state and, therefore, their parents. I came to Hershey High School for revenge. I didn't have a specific plan worked out, but I did know this: it would be public, it would humiliate someone, and it would be clear to that someone that I had orchestrated it.

Call me a planet, orbiting a revenge-colored sun.
Or a seed growing in the gray soil of settling the score.
I am a cold drink, retribution for ice cubes,
a meal spicy with payback.
Call me a film reel. Watch to see what I do.

That's a poem I wrote this summer. I've been writing a lot of poetry since I turned Dark.

As I opened my backpack to put books in my locker, the hall swelled with students and the amplified chatter of the first day. That's when her voice could be heard, sweet and chipper above the rest, a small bird with a sound too big for its body. She pointed to my locker and sang out, "Weirder every year," as the girls trailing her snickered into their palms.

That's Sandy Firestone. And if my heart were a crossbow, every arrow would be aiming at her.

x x x

The sign on my locker read: CELIA THE DARK.

After securing my locker sign with thick strips of duct tape, I made my way to my first-period class, English. English is more than my favorite subject, it's my *only* subject. All other classes are just required credits, but in English, time speeds up, and the bell seems to ring too soon. I've always been a reader. I'm usually involved in at least two books, and I love a library the way the swim team loves towels.

I got to class a minute before the bell and took a seat in the last row. On one side of the room, beneath a bank of windows, were two six-foot tables stacked with novels. Already my heart rate was slowing, and a thin smile was forcing its way onto my face. I took out my notebook and a pen, hoping that class would start with the question, "What books did you read over the summer?"

The teacher walked in carrying a coffee cup and took a seat behind his desk. He was only slightly taller than I was, balding, and his pants were wrinkled. Not the romantic character I hoped for in an English teacher, but I wasn't passing judgment yet.

I was anticipating the bell when a terrible first-day thing happened. Sandy Firestone walked through the door, right behind her best friend and personal tugboat, Mandy Hewton. Yes, their names rhyme. No, this is not a coincidence. In the sixth grade, Mandy went by her full name, Amanda Hewton. In the seventh grade, Amanda climbed the social ladder high enough to score the position of best friend to Sandy and promptly started asking all of our teachers to call her *Mandy*. Despite her new status, Sandy still treats Mandy more like an assistant than an equal, which is obvious to anyone who knows them.

I've known Sandy Firestone since the sixth grade when we both started Hershey Middle School. And by *known*, I do not mean *liked*. To meet Sandy is to understand instantly that she is taking measurement of you in her mind. Her eyes study you before her lips confirm that she considers you either predator or prey. If she considers you prey, meaning you are an ugly girl or a socially awkward boy, then her mouth forms into a pucker like she might be silently saying the word *no*. If she fears you might be a predator, a pretty girl who just moved into the school district or a boy who's smart but uninterested in her, her mouth breaks into a smile wide enough to show two perfect rows of teeth. Sandy did pageants all the way through middle school. That smile got her named Little Miss Derry Township.

Sandy and Mandy plopped down in two open seats on the opposite side of the room, and I tried to force the tiny beads of sweat forming around my hairline back into my skin.

"Ms. Door, hood off please," were my new English teacher's first words to me. *Nice to meet you, too, Mr. Pearson.*

"Okay, students, welcome to ninth-grade Language Arts. Notice I did not say 'English class,' I did not say 'reading' or 'writing class.' I said 'Language Arts class' or 'L.A.' for short. In this class, you won't just be reading books, you will be practicing literary criticism, writing papers, and critiquing one another's work. We will not treat books as things to be passively read and forgotten, but as texts to be analyzed and understood. The first thing we are going to do is get you into your assigned seats."

The same groan goes up every time a teacher says "assigned seats." We groaned the groan.

"Sorry, people, but this is also homeroom, and I don't want to waste a lot of time with attendance, so we're going to do this by alphabet." Oh no. I had been through this before. The last names Door and Firestone are separated by only one letter, and I spent all of eighth-grade English next to Sandy. I could only pray that someone named Susan Edward or David Emanuel was in the classroom. "Cynthia Adams, *here*." Mr. Pearson pointed to a chair at the back, right corner of the room and started working his way forward. "Chad Brooks," he said, "Alicia Brady, Jahlil Cromwell, Anupa Dewan, Celia Door." He pointed to a seat halfway up the row by the windows. I held my breath. *Come on, Susan Edward.* "Sandy Firestone," he continued, "here."

A whole year of Sandy Firestone's blonde hairs on my desk in English class. Clearly, I had been marked by the gods for torment. I sluggishly dragged my boots over and dropped my backpack loudly on my new desk. "Ms. Door, less attitude please," Mr. Pearson responded, giving Sandy the perfect opportunity to smirk as she took her seat in front of me. Sandy squealed when Amanda Hewton ended up in the seat next to her, and they high-fived before wiggling their fingers at each other across the aisle.

I tried to concentrate during the rest of class as we received our syllabus and our first book assignment, *To Kill a Mockingbird* by Harper Lee. But all I thought about was how my year seemed ruined before it had even started. I opened my notebook and tried to console myself the only way I could. *Maybe this wasn't all bad,* I thought. *Maybe this seating arrangement would help provide me with an opportunity to enact my revenge.*

CHAPTER

3

When I say I turned Dark, what I really mean is that I gave up. I gave up on trying to fit in and make everyone like me. I accepted the fact that no one liked me, and I didn't care what they thought. Following the tragic events of my eighth-grade year, I realized that, in a field of sunflowers, I'm a black-eyed Susan.

My Darkness officially began on July 21, the day I turned fourteen. Maybe it didn't *seem* like I changed that much. I didn't become completely gothic and pierce my tongue or dye my hair black. My hair was already dark, and my skin is pretty pasty, but I do wear colors besides black sometimes. Here is a poem I wrote about my skin:

celia's skin
is white like
the sun-bleached bones
of beached whale
skeletons

People pushed me around before I turned Dark, and they still push me around. The difference is that now I push back.

The rest of my first day of high school was bearable. In most classes, our seats were assigned, so I didn't have to worry about who would sit next to me. In French, we were put into groups of three for *conversation*, so I got Liz Thompson and Vanessa Beale, who were now required to talk to me for one class per day. There wasn't much time to kill between periods, and it was easy to look busy at my locker. Lunch, however, was harder to manage. I ventured outside to the grass beyond the basketball court and ate cold pizza with my nose buried in a book. Then I finished the break in the safest, calmest place in every town, school, or jail: the library.

Libraries are my power centers. If I were a character in a video game and my avatar had to go somewhere to recharge her life force after losing a fight, it would be a library. This summer, I devoured two books each week. This fall, I have committed myself to reading at least one book of nonfiction from each of the ten main classes of the Dewey decimal system. If I continue at a rate of one book per week, I'll be finished before Thanksgiving. I would eventually like to read one book from each of the ten divisions of the main classes, and then one book from the ten sections of those ten divisions. But that puts me up to a thousand weeks of reading, or nearly twenty years. That's a lot to undertake at fourteen.

The first day during lunch, I started with the section closest to the doors, which happened to be the Dewey decimal 400s class on language. The librarian looked a little surprised when I checked out *Foreignisms: A Dictionary of Foreign Expressions Commonly (and Not So Commonly) Used in English.*

"Is this part of your language curriculum?" she asked, looking at my school ID card.

"It's not for class," I said back, Darkly. It was the most I said to anyone at school that day in the English language.

The next two days passed without major incident. Sure, on Wednesday morning when I tried raising my hand in English class to say that reading a novel set during the Great Depression was disconcerting in our economic climate, Sandy sighed and said, "Celia, you're so . . . negative."

So I said, "Well, then why don't you take me into a darkroom and see what develops?" which I thought was a clever retort regarding film cameras and photographic negatives.

But then Sandy said, "Ewww, Celia is a lesbian."

So Mr. Pearson said, "Girls, less bickering," and by lunchtime people were calling me Celia the Weird Lesbian.

Still, I was hopeful that high school would allow me

to blend in to a larger pool of oddballs and wallflowers. There had to be enough kids from other feeder middle schools and older grades to let me avoid notice. I dug my trench and prepared to last out the war. It was just after lunch, on Wednesday, that third day of high school that everything changed.

I was doing a locker stop between the library and history, crouched down on one knee, swapping out a novel for a textbook. His voice broke three days of high school quiet. I was so startled, I dropped *European History* right on top of *The Norton Anthology*. "Why does the sign on your locker say 'Celia the Dark'?"

His blue-and-yellow sneakers were a foot from me, their fat laces pouting over the shoes' tongues like bloated earthworms after the rain. One shoe gripped the hallway floor while the other rested its tread casually against a locker. His skinny jeans held his shins as tight as handcuffs and a slim-cut T-shirt embraced his lanky torso under an oversized, orange cotton hoodie. The whole outfit was a dynamic meeting of slender and thick.

He was eating what looked like a burrito from an aluminum foil wrapper, even though we're not allowed to have food outside the lunchroom. And he was gorgeous. I had seen him in the halls and also in my Earth Science class. His name was Drake Berlin, and he had the kind of style that you can achieve only if you were raised in New York City or possibly a foreign country. I knew from science class introductions on the first day that Drake had, in fact, moved here from New York.

A cool, good-looking guy had never approached my locker before. I was half suspicious and half electrified. I tried to sound casual and vaguely menacing. "Because I'm Dark," I said, picking up my history text again.

Drake said something that none of my classmates had said to me in a long time. He said, "That's cool." Then he added, "Do you like comic books?" and popped the last of the burrito into his mouth.

That day after school, Drake and I went to the wooded lot for the first time.

The town of Hershey, Pennsylvania, was built in 1903 by Milton S. Hershey to house workers at his chocolate factory. The tagline for Hershey is "The Sweetest Place on Earth," but it should be "A Town Dedicated to the Worship of Refined Sugar." Half of the kids in my school have been diagnosed with attention deficit disorder, and all the kids in my school are being pumped full of Hershey's chocolate from morning until night.

Drake's grandmother lives in the same subdivision as my family. It's the sort of planned community that has five model homes to pick from, and the only big choice the homebuyer faces is whether to get a one-car garage or two. My house is model number 3: the Cape Cod. My dad used to drive around the neighborhood pointing out the other Cape Cods and naming the families who picked them. "Look, Steve Bishop got a Cape Cod, too," he would point out to my mother. "Even with one story, I still think it's the best use of the square footage."

My mom would generally respond with something

like, "Which night is Celia's parent/teacher conference?" My parents often sounded like two people who were not involved in the same conversation. It was like they were each talking to someone else on a cell phone with one of those invisible headsets, but they happened to be looking at each other while they did it.

Drake's grandmother's house wasn't one of the five models. It was the house that sat on the land before the subdivision came, so it lived at the end of one of our cul-de-sacs like an apple tree in an orchard full of peaches. It's the only house adjacent to undeveloped land.

As we walked the cleanly edged sidewalks from school to our neighborhood, Drake explained. "My grandparents moved to Hershey from New York City so they could retire someplace quiet. When they built their house, this was all trees," he said, using his hand gesture like a chain saw to cut down the row of houses we were passing. "Developers bought the plots around the house, and Gran says the trees came down like dominos, and the houses came up like dandelions, and now they live in the middle of a development with only one lot full of trees. Developers still call her every year to ask if she wants to sell it."

Ever since Drake and I left school, I had been fidgeting awkwardly with my clothing. I kept pulling on my hood and taking it off again. I was tugging the string of my hoodie first all the way down with my right hand and then all the way down with my left. It was like I was trying to saw off my head at the neck with a soft cotton blade. I forced myself to release the hoodie string and say something to the beautiful, articulate boy who was walking next to me.

"Do you . . . like Hershey?" I inquired robotically. Bingo. I went right to the top of the most boring questions list. I actually winced after the words left my mouth.

"Krackel and Special Dark miniatures, yes," said Drake. "The town, not so much."

When we got to Drake's house, we circumnavigated the front lawn of his grandmother's one-story rancher and went straight to the wooded lot beyond her manicured backyard. We walked until the canopy became dense, and after some careful climbing around in underbrush, found a downed tree to sit on like a bench. It was a nurse log, meaning it was dead, but new, smaller trees were using it as fertilizer to grow from. I read about nurse logs in a book called *Nights in the Forest*. The air smelled sweet and wet back there, and the normal neighborhood sounds—televisions, passing cars, barking dogs—were replaced by birds, squirrels, and snapping twigs.

I was wearing black leggings with black boots. I pulled my hood all the way up so it covered part of my face and then I wrapped my arms around my legs and hugged them. I acted like I was feeling chilly, but really I felt vulnerable. Immediately, Drake asked the question I feared.

"Who are your friends at school?" He asked it casually, like it was a "getting to know you question."

"Um," I said, and instantly my voice was too high. Not even a full word out of my mouth on the subject of friendship and I was blowing it. I tried to follow with another sound at a lower pitch, but my voice disappeared altogether and then my throat was as empty as an abandoned coalmine.

"Why did you move here from New York City?" I asked, acting like the question had occurred to me suddenly.

Drake got up from the log and walked over to a tree with low-hanging branches. After testing a limb with half his weight, he placed one fat sneaker in the branch's shoulder and stood all the way up next to the trunk.

"I screwed up," he said from the tree. "You have to apply to get into high school in New York, and I want to go to an arts school and do illustration. I picked out my top three schools and made my portfolio, but I got my application in late, and now everything is full. My parents feel bad that they weren't on top of it, so they are trying to get it straightened out," he said, placing his sneaker on the next branch up, "but I have to stay with Gran and go to Hershey High in the meantime or else go to the school I'm zoned for, which is basically a nightmare." He pulled himself up again to a higher branch.

I knew about the horrors of school zoning. I had the same group of four friends all the way through elementary school: Jane, Emily, Raisa, and Sarabeth. Every Friday night of fourth and fifth grade, one of us hosted a sleepover, and everyone else was invited. We traveled as such a pack that if my dad saw just two of us together, he would say, "Where's the rest of the herd?" But in fifth grade, the school board changed the map, and I got zoned to go to Hershey Middle School while everyone else was zoned for Hilltop.

We still played together the summer after fifth grade, and I got invited to their birthday parties in sixth. But when they talked about the teacher who blew spit bubbles when he talked, I couldn't laugh along. And the name *Chad* did not make me jump onto the nearest bed and giggle. I was out of the loop, and after a while, our unbreakable bonds of friendship broke. Hilltop Middle is zoned for Lower Dauphin High School, Hershey High's primary rival, so I might see them again if I could stomach going to the homecoming game at the start of October. There were signs for it all over the halls at school.

"So, you might just be in Hershey for ninth grade?" I asked.

"Hopefully, I'll only be in Hershey a *month*!" He laughed from up in the tree. "I'm on the wait list for two schools, and the admissions offices said that something could open up in the first thirty days. I'm not really living here," he added, tugging on a higher limb with both hands. "Just visiting."

I didn't realize that my hope had gotten itself up and

brushed itself off until it got knocked down into the dirt again. He was just visiting. Figures.

"I can see why you don't have a lot of friends here," Drake added, testing the same limb with his foot. "The kids in this town are too lame to get you." He stepped again into the next higher foothold of the tree, and I couldn't see his face anymore between the branches.

There were two butterflies flirting with each other above a bush several feet away. The hood slipped off my head as I looked up to where Drake was climbing. A limb shook as his feet disappeared fully into the tree.

5

Before Drake went inside for dinner, he turned to me and yelled, "See you tomorrow at school." I kept replaying those words in my head as I walked home. *At school*, reverberated at the end of each line, the way a bell keeps singing for a few seconds after you ring it.

As usual, my mom wasn't home. At least three nights a week she works the swing shift from two p.m. until ten p.m., which is the only reliable thing in her schedule. As one of the newest nurses at the hospital, she has to fill in as shifts come up, so sometimes she works the night shift until six a.m. and then sleeps for a few hours before going in for a swing. She works in the pediatric unit. The most consistent thing about seeing my mom is that you can count on her to look tired.

She left a note:

You can eat pasta or grilled cheese.
Your sheets are still in the dryer.
Please be in bed by ten p.m.

My mother's communications are becoming so spare, they are turning into poems. I edited the note to make it a haiku.

pasta or grilled cheese.
your sheets are in the dryer.
bed by ten p.m.

I was never home alone like this before Dad left. My parents are currently involved in a "trial separation" that officially began in July when my dad separated all the way to Atlanta. I wanted to go with him but was forced to stay here in Hershey with a mom who works all the time. They didn't even say, "Get ready to be kicked out of the nest, baby bird." The nest just flipped over one day, and I'm left trying to fly on my own. Naturally, I have a refrigerator door full of emergency numbers, instructions on dealing with everything from a fire to a snake bite, and three neighbors ready to come to my rescue if a creepy, unmarked van should so much as drive down the street.

Grabbing some cold pasta from the fridge, I went down the hall to my room to check for email from Dorathea. I set the pasta down on my desk and forgot to eat any. There was a drummer keeping time in my head and the bass drum sounded like *Drake, Drake, Drake.* My inbox offered no new emails from Dorathea to distract me.

Dorathea is my only cousin. She's in her sophomore year at University of California, Berkeley, and she is like my own personal Magic 8 Ball. I go to her when I need mystical answers with questionable reliability. I decided to send another email, even though I wrote last. I hoped that didn't make me look needy.

Re: question

From: Celia (celia@celiathedark.com)

Sent: Wed 9/08 6:42 PM

To: Dorathea Eberhardt (deberhardt@berkeley.edu)

hey, dorathea,

when a guy comes up to you at your locker and asks if you want to hang out in a wooded lot after school, and then tells you that you are too cool for the kids in your town, does it mean he likes you or that he wants to be your friend?

how's college?

celia

I want Dorathea to think I'm cool. Maybe that's lame to admit, but she's the one person reasonably close to my age who doesn't consider me a loser. Of course, I never told her about what happened in the eighth grade. I never told anyone.

Turning away from the computer, I flopped onto my

bed and reached one hand into the cool, dark recesses below my mattress. I like to think of my bed as a house and the space beneath it as the basement. Down there in the cellar, nestling at the base of the nightstand where I left it, was my notebook.

In the case of fire and a mad scramble to run from the flames, there is no contest among my possessions for the honor of "item to be saved first." Poetry notebook wins. My only problem would be deciding which one. I have three notebooks full and am scribbling my way through number four. Most are standard composition books, their black-and-white-marbled covers eroded by stickers, traced Manga drawings, and quotes from famous people written in marker. My current notebook says, "'Great things are not accomplished by those who yield to trends and fads and popular opinion.'—Charles Kuralt."

I write poetry every day. Sometimes people think poetry has to be obscure or complicated or spring forth directly from your soul with the magical force of nature. I think poetry is like music—you either like to make it or you don't.

I pulled out my notebook and wrote this poem:

I expected you to vanish
up and up into the tree,
a shake of the branches
and gone like you

had never happened.
But you came down
and handed me a leaf
"from seven limbs up,
already yellow," you said,
and then you walked away
and you were still real.

I took the yellow leaf out of my hoodie pocket and pressed it between the pages of my notebook. Then I lay on my bed trying to read. It was two more hours until my heart slowed down enough to let me fall asleep.

CHAPTER

6

Thursday, the day after I met Drake, I showed up for school with a beehive buzzing in my brain. Would he talk to me again? Had he somehow discovered that I was an outcast? Was he a hallucination brought on by my extreme loneliness, an imaginary friend created by my subconscious to protect me? I went to my locker to get my book before English and as soon as I unlocked the door, a note fell out. Someone must have stuffed it in through the air vents. *A note from Drake?* I hopefully snatched the folded paper from the floor and opened it. It said:

You're not fooling anyone, Weird. You're still a loser.

I did not let my shoulders fall or inhale too sharply. I didn't display any identifiable sign of suffering. In high school, it's not just the walls that have eyes. The lockers, lunch tables, and desks have ears and gossiping mouths.

Naturally, my first guess about who wrote the note

was that pit bull Sandy Firestone or one of her pack of mongrels. Sandy had had a group of freshman girls trailing her since school started, and so far, I had made it through three days with no visible bite marks from their canines, so they had to be thirsting for my blood by now. But the longer I looked at the note, the more it didn't seem like Sandy's work. The handwriting was sloppy, and I can say from brutal experience that Sandy and her hounds are more cunning and vicious than an anonymous locker note.

Like my neighbor's cat, Peaches, who drops dead mice on our front porch after tormenting them to death all night, Sandy toys with her prey. In seventh grade, I overheard her talking to Becky Shapiro in the girls' bathroom. I was in one of the stalls.

"Becky," said Sandy, who had been standing at the mirror applying makeup since I walked into the bathroom.

"Yeah?" said Becky, turning off her faucet and sounding surprised that Sandy was addressing her.

Becky Shapiro was overweight. In the sixth grade, she had to have a special table at school instead of a chair with a desk attached like the rest of us. She couldn't fit into a fixed desk.

"Me and some of the girls were talking, and we think you should try the Atkins diet," said Sandy offhandedly as if she were offering advice to a friend who asked for it.

I heard Becky let out a long sigh as she tore off a paper towel.

"Well, I'm sorry, Becky," Sandy went on, clearly offended by Becky's response, "but you need to do something. It's kind of . . . *depressing*," Sandy finished, like she had been searching around for the saddest sort of word she could find.

That happened a year before Sandy started using me as a sharpening stone for her claws. I hadn't turned Dark yet. I stayed in the stall longer than necessary and tried not to make any noise.

Next, Becky said something that made my heart sound like a broken wind chime. She said, "You're right, Sandy . . . thanks."

And as if things had been restored to their proper order, Sandy said, "You're welcome," and snapped shut the lid on her lipstick tube.

The piece of folded paper that I was currently holding featured too much anonymity to be created by Sandy Firestone. Sandy liked to take credit for her brutality.

"Did you get a love note?" said a voice in my ear.

I was startled and balled up the paper, crushing it beneath the black nails of my right fist.

"Sorry," said Drake, his brown eyes brimming with honesty. "I didn't mean to scare you."

I stared back at him without a word to say.

"Hey, um," said Drake, kicking his sneaker gently against the wall below the lockers, "do you want to eat lunch together today?"

I tossed the note back into my locker like it was a trash can. "Sure," I said back, slamming the door.

CHAPTER

7

That afternoon, a momentous event occurred. For the first time since high school started four days ago, I didn't eat lunch by myself. The day was so warm, it felt more like August outside than September. After we picked a spot on the grass near the basketball court, Drake pulled off his sweater, but I kept wearing my black hoodie. I like having a hood at my fingertips.

I was also wearing black tights and combat boots with a polyester dress my mom handed down to me. It looked like something a 1970s housewife would wear to host a holiday party, offering her guests drinks in ceramic tiki cups. I had cut it off so it would hang just above my knees.

For lunch, I brought the pasta I didn't finish from the night before, and Drake had a turkey sub. I could feel the eyes of the high school wandering over us, the new kid and the outcast eating their lunches in the grass. Frankly, I was as mystified by Drake's interest in me as my classmates probably were. New kids at school always have to work to make friends, but Drake was cool and good looking. He could have tried to get into one of the big, jovial groups populating the picnic tables. Why pick a loner? Did Drake want to go out with me? Was this turkey-and-pasta brown bag our first lunch date?

I slipped on a pair of dark sunglasses and tried not to betray my confusion. We had barely swallowed our first bites before the boys started gathering on the basketball court. I don't know how boys can eat so fast.

"Do they always play a pickup game now?" asked Drake, leaning back on one elbow on the grass to get a better view of the court.

"I've seen them out here the past three days," I said.

"Can anyone join?" he asked, as if I was an insider on the Hershey sports scene.

"I dunno," I said, but Drake's question was answered when the tallest boy on the court filled with seven guys yelled, "Anybody else?" in the general direction of the picnic tables.

Drake's eyes scanned the court like he was speed-reading a book. He appeared to be calculating something.

"Are you into basketball?" I asked.

"Yeah," Drake said without taking his eyes off the players. "In New York I played all the time."

Oh yeah, New York. My joy turned sour. I was sharing my lunch with someone for the first time in high school, and he was staying only a month. Whatever was happening between Drake and me, it was temporary.

"I'm going to get in on this game," Drake said suddenly, practically jumping up to a full stand from where he was reclining on the grass. "Watch my stuff?" He bounded over to the courts as I picked his sweater up out of the grass and put the rest of his sub back in his lunch bag.

Drake entered the game just as team selection was starting. A couple of the other boys gave him lazy half waves and I could almost read their lips mumbling, "What's up, man?" Drake's shoulders slouched when he was with the other boys, and he kept his hands in his pockets. It was like they were all competing to see who could look the most disinterested. Some mysterious ritual involving gestures toward players and baskets was followed by a jump shot, and then the game was on.

The only other boy I recognized on the court was Joey Gaskill, another ninth grader who went to my middle school. Since I first met him in the sixth grade, I've watched the spill of menace that leaks from Joey grow larger with each year. In sixth grade, he got suspended for fighting. In seventh, he was suspended again after he snuck into a math room during lunch and set a stack of tests on fire, tripping the sprinkler system and ruining books and electronics in an entire wing of the building. In eighth grade, someone broke into the ceramics room one night and smashed all the green pots waiting to be fired in the kiln. No one could prove that Joey did it, but everyone seemed to share the unshakable assurance that it was him.

I was shocked to see Joey playing a team sport. I was even more shocked to see that he was wearing a Hershey High basketball jersey, indicating that he had made the JV team.

From the start, Drake was impressive. I know nothing about basketball, but when one player keeps getting the ball and running with it, it's pretty obvious he's a talent. Drake made two baskets while I watched. The scene inspired me to write. I was experimenting with visual poetry.

BASKETBALL
boys grunt and shuffle
check right then left and sweat,
grit their pounding teeth as the earth
keeps grabbing the ball back. they are
practicing to be jackhammers. they are
practicing to be men, looking for
something they can win.
basketball

I was so involved in writing my poem, I didn't notice Sandy and Mandy approaching until they spread out a blanket in the grass near me with a crew of four girls I didn't know from middle school. Social-climbing transfer students maybe, or mean girls from other feeder schools. A chilly wind blew from their direction. I pulled my hood up and stuck my nose farther into my journal to pretend I was still working on my poem.

"I think she got that dress from her grandmother." I heard Mandy's voice carry over, followed by a smattering of laughter. "And it was already out of style when her grandmother wore it."

"She thinks she's alternative," responded Sandy, "when really she's just gross. She smells like a junk shop."

"She smells like a Dumpster," echoed Mandy.

"Did you see the sign she put on her locker?" said a third girl's voice.

I had to force myself not to glance over at them. The space between us on the grass folded together like an accordion. They were inches away instead of feet. I could feel them breathing on me.

"Look at her writing in her journal. She thinks she's so much deeper than the rest of us. I'm sure people are lining up to read books by fringy, high school creepers," said Sandy.

I could feel my face starting to flush and glanced up to make sure Drake wasn't noticing anything. He was still involved with the game. I was writing so hard in my notebook, I poked my pen tip through a few pages. I thought they couldn't affect me anymore. When I turned Dark, I thought I stopped letting Sandy get to me. It was starting to feel like eighth grade all over again, like there was a black hole opening up in my chest with enough gravity to suck me into it.

"Maybe she's in love with the new guy," said Mandy.

"As if someone that hot would date someone that ugly," Sandy came back.

"He probably ate lunch with her so she would do his homework," said another girl I didn't know.

One of the by-products of mean high school girls is other mean high school girls. Even though two of the girls who were talking about me didn't even know me, ganging up on another girl is the quickest way to get into the gang.

I wanted to get up and leave. But leaving would be like sending them a note that said, "Dear Mandy and Sandy, I submit to your dominant power." Ice formed between my butt and the grass, holding me frozen in place. I just kept writing in my poetry book and pretending I didn't hear them. In actuality, my hearing had become five times better. I could hear them click their fake nails together like claws.

When the bell rang, Mandy and Sandy's group stood to leave. Sandy threw one last comment at me over her shoulder, as if she were littering. "Drake told me he was going to hang with her because he feels sorry for her."

I looked down at my poetry notebook. My "poem" read:

things celia needs to change
things celia needs to change

things celia needs to change
things celia needs to change
things celia needs to change
things celia needs to change
things celia needs to change

CHAPTER

8

After the basketball game, Drake asked me to go to the wooded lot again after school. I spent the next three periods failing to sit still in class. I must have asked to go to the bathroom or water fountain twenty times before the final bell. I was so drunk on the thrill of discovering him, I managed to forget about what Sandy and Mandy did at lunch. Drake was from a fantasy world called New York City, a place where it was possible that people might actually "get me." If I was an alien here, then Drake had come from my home world, and we were both currently stranded on a bizarre planet called Pennsylvania.

"Meet anyone cool in the basketball game?" I asked on the walk home, trying to sound nonchalant.

Drake cleared his throat. "Yeah, one of the guys told me about the new exhibit at the art gallery, and another one invited me to a silent film festival." He looked at me and crossed his eyes. He was carrying his skateboard under one arm so we could walk together.

"Oh yeah, those guys never shut up about the symphony season," I managed to say before hiding my hot cheeks inside my hood. I was still holding out hope that I might have fooled this hapless newcomer into believing I was one of the cool people in Hershey, not some jealous girl desperate for friends.

"All the jocks love Debussy," Drake said back.

When we got to his house, we cut across his lawn to the wooded lot. I followed Drake through the leafy ground cover and snarling undergrowth to the same horizontal log we had populated the day before. It felt familiar to me already as we each settled in across from each other on a smooth and barkless section of the tree trunk.

The more time I was spending with Drake, the more I found myself noticing how truly handsome he was. When he smiled, his jaw formed a set of ninety-degree angles, and his mouth sat in the middle like it was framed. He had brown eyes and exceptionally long eyelashes for a boy. His hair was styled to point up in the middle, a short faux-hawk. Drake's lips, particularly the bottom one, were plump. If you sat close enough, you could count the creases in the pulpy flesh. I counted fourteen, sitting on the log.

"Celia," he said, snapping me out of my crease-counting daze. I turned away from him to fumble awk-wardly in my backpack, so I had an excuse to hide my face. "Yeah?" I responded distantly. I pulled lip balm out of my bag and made a show of putting it on.

"So, do you date guys or girls?" asked Drake. "Or both?"

He asked me casually like we were talking about bowling. "Still using duckpins?" he might have been saying. "Or have you graduated to ten-pin bowling?"

"Um, I guess . . . guys," I answered, trying to match his casual tone. I hesitated because in order to date guys, you actually have to go *on dates*. I had never been on an *actual* date.

I do have an interest in guys. In fact, I have so many love interests, I've organized them by genre. My classic crush is Mr. Darcy from *Pride and Prejudice*. For fantasy, I've chosen Aragorn from Lord of the Rings. Sci-fi is a tie between Peeta and Gale from *The Hunger Games*, and my favorite contemporary fiction bad boy is Holden Caulfield from *The Catcher in the Rye*. Maybe they aren't exactly real boys, but I feel like I know them all, their deepest thoughts and desires. It's not like I'm going to go get a crush on some boy in Hershey High when I've got Howl from *Howl's Moving Castle* at home.

I wasn't about to tell any of that to Drake, though, and I didn't know why was he asking me. Was he checking my sexual preference before telling me he liked me? Was this a New York thing? I held my breath to listen for what Drake would say next, hoping he would ask me out or ask me to be his girlfriend or whatever boys ask when they like you.

"Well, I . . . like guys," Drake said in a voice that

sounded abrupt and professional. Then he softened and added, "*A guy*, actually."

I was suddenly aware of all the little noises around me. There was the textured, white noise of the leaves rustling and falling, at least three types of birds calling to one another from high branches, the distant hum of the highway. It had never crossed my mind that Drake might like boys. There were two older men at my church who were a couple, but I had never met anyone my age who was gay.

Drake stood up off the log, put his hands on his head, and said, "Wow. That felt *so* good." He wiped his palms off on his jeans like they had been sweating. "I have never said those words out loud to anyone before."

The best response I could come up with was, "Um . . . congratulations."

"Thanks, Celia," he said sincerely, putting a hand onto his chest. "I needed a test run. I needed to tell someone who just met me, who I knew wouldn't judge me. I've been nervous about it all day."

I sat on the nurse log trying not to wish he had said something else. I kept crossing and uncrossing my legs, looking for a position that didn't seem awkward.

"I just feel like it's time now." Drake started to walk carefully over the roots around the log. "Ninth grade, high school, new opportunity to define yourself." Drake used his hands to talk. "I wanted to tell someone before I go back to New York this weekend and come out for real."

"*For real?*"

"You know, like tell the people who really know me. My parents and Japhy." Drake sat back down on the log next to me.

I reminded myself for the second time that day that Drake's real life was still back in New York. "Japhy?" I asked. "Like the character in *Dharma Bums?*"

"Hippie parents." Drake laughed. "His mom's an actress at the theatre my dad runs. You're well read."

"Is Japhy *the guy?*"

"Yeah. He's *the guy*. He's my best friend since we were ten. We've always been close, and I guess I always knew I had feelings, but in the last month . . . I don't know, something's been changing. You know, Celia, when you can just *tell* someone likes you?"

"Yeah. It's so . . . cool when that happens," I lied.

"The last time he was over . . ." Drake stopped. "It's hard to explain."

"Do you guys hang out a lot?" I didn't want to feel jealous of Drake's other friend, his *best* friend, whom he did *like*. But I did.

"Our parents have always had dinner together every Tuesday night and then gone to a show. When we were little, they would bring Japhy over and get us a sitter. When we turned twelve, we convinced them we could be left alone. Well, really, Japhy convinced them. Japhy likes trouble."

Since I met Drake the day before, he had looked so confident and unflappable. Now he was blushing and braiding his fingers together. He stood up again and picked a stick out of the dirt.

"When we do something risky, or a little dangerous, Japhy calls it the 'envelope,' like 'Come on man, we gotta *push the envelope.*'" Drake kicked leaves away from a patch of dirt and started drawing pictures with his stick. I dangled a leg on either side of our tree-bench.

"Sometimes we sneak out and go to Times Square, talk to homeless guys, skateboard on subway platforms, count rats." Drake drew a circle surrounded by arrows. "Our parents don't know about any of it."

Jealousy threatened to burn a hole right through my sweatshirt. Why didn't I get a best friend to sneak out of the house and count rats with? Why didn't I get a best friend who was possibly in love with me and liked trouble? I felt cheated. Sandy Firestone's face flashed through my mind.

"But the last time, we decided to stay home. We were playing video games in the living room, and I kept beating him. So, finally, he grabbed the controller out of my hand and tackled me. Japhy's athletic, great at basketball and skating. I was fighting back, but he pinned me on the floor." Drake threw down his stick and stood in the leaves, holding out both arms to pantomime the act of holding someone down. "We've always wrestled, but this time when he was lying on top of me, he just looked at me and smiled. Then he said, 'Don't beat me again,' and got up." Drake's cheeks were in full bloom, red as a sunburn.

"After that, we just sat on the fire escape and watched pedestrians. But I have the feeling that he was telling me something. That smile. Wow, I'm so nervous," Drake said, shaking his hands like he had just washed them and couldn't find a towel.

"There's a new play opening at my dad's theatre this weekend. I'll see it Friday night, and then Japhy will come over Saturday night while our parents are at the show again. I'm going to tell him, Celia. Or, at least, see how things go and maybe tell him or maybe just . . . No. I have to tell him. I can't chicken out." Drake ran both hands through his hair and then styled it again. "Then I'll tell my parents on Sunday.

"Celia," said Drake, turning toward me and folding both arms over his chest. "Promise me you won't tell anyone what I told you? I don't want anyone in Hershey to know before I tell my parents."

Drake looked so vulnerable then, I felt terrible for being jealous of him. Plus, it had been a painfully long time since anyone shared a secret with me. "Drake," I said, pulling my hands out of my hoodie sleeves and clutching them together. "I would never do that. I promise I won't tell anyone."

"Thanks," said Drake, moving to sit down next to me

on the log again. "Okay, your turn. Now you have to tell me something."

I swear I almost told Drake right then, all about eighth grade and Sandy and the Book. It was the perfect moment with a secret hanging out on my tongue just waiting to sprout wings and fly out of my mouth. But a familiar black hole started to open in my chest sucking my words away into it. What if I told him the truth and he didn't like me anymore? He was staying for only a month, but a friend for a month was better than no friend at all. I needed him too much to be honest with him.

"I write poetry," I blurted out.

"Oh, cool," said Drake, sounding only mildly disappointed with my tame secret. "Will you read it to me sometime?"

A little light started to flicker in my chest where the black hole had been. I nodded.

Before I left his house to walk home, Drake asked me if I wanted to walk to school together the next day. So, Friday morning, the end of our first week of ninth grade, I showed up at the park in our neighborhood at eight a.m. I was there a few minutes early, hoping to get to school in time to exchange my library book before first period. I hadn't read all of *Foreignisms* because it was a bit like reading the phone book, but I did pick up some good words and felt I could ethically move on to the 500s class of the Dewey decimal system. I sat on a swing to wait for Drake.

I don't have a cell phone. I had one, briefly, when my dad left for Atlanta and bought me one, saying we could "keep in touch better." But I left it in my hoodie pocket and accidentally washed it and that was the end of my connectivity. Mom said, "No more cell phone until you make enough money to replace that one. You're old enough to babysit." This particular attempt to teach me responsibility reeked of hypocrisy because she loses things more than anyone. Since the only people who called me were my mom and dad, I decided to teach a lesson of my own and not bother to earn money for a replacement. Now my dad mostly emails, and my mom has to deal with not being able to contact me whenever she wants.

Waiting for Drake in the park, I checked the time on the digital watch I got at the thrift store. It told me Drake was running late. I started pushing my feet back and letting myself swing casually forward, then twirling side to side, looking down the street in the direction of Drake's house and then up the street toward school. At ten minutes after eight, I started to get a bad feeling. Maybe I didn't react well enough to Drake being gay. Maybe he was hoping that I was gay, too, and now that he knew I wasn't, he wasn't all that interested in me. Maybe he just wanted someone to practice coming out to and I had served my purpose. It's not like it really mattered, since he was going back to New York soon anyway, and I would go back to being a lone wolf again, no friend in sight.

I used to have a best friend in middle school, from sixth to eighth grade. Ruth and I found each other at the public library the weekend after school started, both reading *The Egypt Game* on a sunny Saturday afternoon. We fell into a conversation about the book and didn't climb out of it for two hours.

Ruth's family was religious, and she wasn't allowed to watch television or wear pants. She wore long white dresses and a blonde braid that hung to her waist. She also wasn't allowed to have sleepovers or go to the mall, so our friendship, although intensely close, was limited.

One of the ways we connected was by reading the same book and trying to stay on the same page so that neither one of us gave away plot points. Sometimes she would call to say, "I couldn't stop myself and I read a hundred more pages after dinner." I would have to stay up late to catch up. One time I was so sick with the flu that I couldn't hold up a book, and Ruth read to me over the phone from *James and the Giant Peach* for over an hour until I fell asleep with the receiver on my pillow.

We were inseparable at school and good students. But middle school is a toxic environment for kids who deviate from the mainstream. Maybe it was my friendship with Ruth that first brought me to the attention of Sandy Firestone. Early in the seventh grade, Ruth was targeted. Changing in the locker room before gym, she pulled off her button-down dress, revealing large, white cotton panties that looked two sizes too big, and a heavy, stitched polyester bra. They seemed out of place on her body, like a three-piece suit on the beach.

Ruth was already starting to "develop," so she needed the polyester bra. What little I have in the boob department hadn't started to emerge yet, so I was still wearing an undershirt.

"Jesus, Ruth," said Sandy Firestone from her station at the lockers. "Do you even have hand-me-down underwear?"

Mandy was still vying to be Sandy's favorite back then, so she laughed like she was at a comedy club. They were both wearing matching bra-and-panty sets and taking their time before they put on their gym shorts.

Ruth looked like she wanted her locker to be a portal to another world so she could climb in and climb out in Narnia. That was before I turned Dark, so instead of saying anything, I just put my head in my locker and hoped Sandy wouldn't notice me. These sorts of attacks went on for weeks.

Ruth made some desperate attempts to fit in. She would fly into the bathroom as soon as she got to school and emancipate her hair from the braid snaking down her shoulder blade. I learned to replicate it for her at the end of the day so that her hair didn't betray its daily freedom when her mom picked her up. She rolled up the sleeves of her dresses in a sad attempt to look more urban and worked at opening up more, smiling and even chatting with people other than me. Still, we didn't manage to attract any more close friends. We were an oddball couple of library nerds who made easy shooting for Sandy and Mandy.

But Ruth and I were happy hanging out after school. We played in our imaginations, invented new worlds, and spent hours sketching characters who lived there. Ruth was the third oldest of seven brothers and sisters, so at her house, we were constantly interrupted to change diapers or make someone a snack. At my house, Ruth reveled in the quiet, with my mom studying for nursing school and my dad always coming home late.

It was in the spring of eighth grade when Ruth's mom came to pick her up from school early one Friday for a church retreat. She found Ruth talking to me at my locker with her dress unbuttoned and her hair hanging in spirals around her face, eye shadow brushed onto both lids. As Ruth's mother grabbed her hand and snapped her head toward the nearest exit, her own braid cast out like a whip. She didn't let Ruth get her things from her locker or say good-bye. She just wrenched her from the clutches of public school like she was pulling her from the arms of Satan. Ruth held one hand out toward me like I might have a life ring to throw her. I didn't.

I tried to call. Ruth's mother answered both times, and the second time, she asked me politely not to call back. I got a letter in the mail a week later. Ruth wrote that she was going to be homeschooled from now on and that she wasn't allowed to talk to me anymore.

I appealed to my parents for help. My dad said, "I'm sorry, Celia, but we can't tell anyone else how to raise their children." My mom twisted a finger in her curly hair and sighed, "Maybe her parents will change their minds. It's painful, but sometimes a friendship just has to end." They both seemed distracted. I read *Bridge to Terabithia* and cried every night, wishing the phone would ring. Two weeks later, my parents told me they were separating, and three weeks after that was the incident with the Book.

I was sitting on the park swing, thinking about Ruth and wondering if I would ever see her again, when Drake finally appeared twenty minutes late, pushing himself fast down the street on a skateboard. He skidded to a stop on the sidewalk closest to the swing set and stepped on one end of his board, grabbing the other with his hand.

"Dude, I'm so sorry. I overslept," he said, running a hand through his hair and then attempting to force it into a style with his fingers.

"No big deal." I shrugged, hoisting myself out of the hammock-like swing and disguising a relieved sigh. Drake had shown up; he hadn't disappeared or decided he didn't like me or been dragged away by a parent to be home-schooled. We walked as quickly as possible the twenty blocks to school.

I slid into my desk for first-period Language Arts moments after the bell and received a warning glare from Mr. Pearson. From the desk ahead of mine, Sandy muttered, "Spend too much time deciding which black skirt to wear today?" Mandy, next to her, nearly choked with laughter.

"It's probably easy to be on time when you are unburdened by creative impulses," I said back in an agreeable tone.

"Yeah, that's why everyone hates you Celia, it's because you're such a creative genius," spat Mandy, defending her hero.

"Sarcasm is the lowest form of wit," I hissed back, although I'm sure my Oscar Wilde quote was lost on Mandy.

She appeared to be prepping a counterattack when Mr. Pearson told us bluntly to be quiet and get out our books. Getting the last word with Sandy or Mandy would likely ensure a more vicious attack from them later, but I still relished the triumph for the remainder of class.

The rest of the school day was uneventful. No more

locker notes or girl-on-girl hazing. Drake and I ate lunch outside, and he played impressively in the pickup game. I spent European History and math working on a poem I was writing about how braiding hair is like making pretzels out of dough. When the last bell finally rang, I was standing at my locker waiting for Drake when two terrible things happened.

First, Clock materialized, dressed, as always, in a black trench coat. Clock's real name is Daniel, and his last name is Kloch, which most people assume rhymes with "blotch," but really sounds like "clock." I know because we had classes together in middle school, and every time we had a new teacher or a substitute, she would attempt to call out his name on the attendance sheet before he tensely corrected her by saying, "Clock, just call me Clock." I never saw one teacher insist on calling him Daniel. Clock was always quiet and brooding, but in seventh grade he started going for the full, hungry vampire look. I think he even shades in half-moons under his eyes with makeup.

Clock was sliding down the hall in a gothic saunter when he noticed me. Clock didn't really talk to me in middle school. But now that we were both freshman fish in the big, scary pond of upperclassmen sharks, I wondered if he might acknowledge me. Unfortunately, he did.

"Get the note I left you, Weird?" he taunted as he walked past, his black combat boots thudding on the buffed linoleum.

Despite my Darker instincts, my mouth hung open. As outcasts and freaks, Clock and I should have been natural allies. But in the chaotic battleground of high school, he had chosen to be my enemy. I couldn't believe he was the one who left the note.

I shot back, "Don't you have a vampire romance to read?"

"Wow," he countered. "Finally grew a pair for high school. New boyfriend making you braver?" Then he was off, the tail of his black coat disappearing down the hall and into a crowd of students.

Boyfriend? What made Clock say that? Do other people think Drake is my boyfriend? I didn't have a lot of time to ponder the issue. If Clock's comments stung me like a jellyfish, then what happened next had the poisonous barb of a manta ray.

I looked down the hall to see Drake walking toward me. Clutching Drake's arm at the elbow and grinning like he was her escort to a cotillion was Sandy Firestone. Catching sight of my face through the crowd, Sandy tugged at Drake's arm to make him stop. Then she stood on both of her tiptoes, pressed her body along the length of Drake's side, and cupped a hand around her mouth to whisper in his ear.

Drake seemed unaware that I was watching them. Sandy was not. After finishing her personal game of telephone, Sandy giggled once at Drake and then ran off down the hall. I bitterly regretted pissing Sandy off in first period. I spun around before Drake could catch me looking and tried with all of my lungs to catch my breath. I swallowed two bellyfuls of air before Drake made it to my locker.

"Ready for your bodyguard to get you safely out of the building, pop star?" Drake asked when he reached me.

Despite all the stings I was nursing, I forced a smile. "The water in my limo better be ice cold this time"—I shut the door to my locker—"or heads will roll."

"I think I'm doing the right thing. Do you think I'm doing the right thing? He likes me, right? I'm pretty sure he likes me. It feels like now is the right time, but maybe I should wait." Drake's internal debate club dominated the conversation on our walk home from school.

I wasn't responding much because I couldn't stop thinking about Drake talking to Sandy. I almost asked him what they were saying to each other approximately forty-seven times, but I knew it would come out sounding jealous. I was glad I hadn't told him about the eighth grade, about my stomach-growling desire for revenge. How could I trust him now that he was talking to the enemy?

"Just be honest," I advised hypocritically. "Who wouldn't like you?" When we got to the park in our neighborhood, we exchanged phone numbers—cell for Drake, landline for me—and IM names before parting for the weekend.

"Gran's waiting to drive me to Harrisburg—train for New York leaves at six." Drake got on his skateboard. "Wish me luck."

"Good luck," I said with tepid enthusiasm as he rolled down the sidewalk away from me.

When I walked into my house, I was not shocked to find my mom on the phone. My aunt Alyce, Dorathea's mom, lives in Oregon, and she and my uncle got a divorce a few years ago. Breaking up with your husband must give you a lot of stuff to talk about, because my mom and my aunt have been on the phone every day since my dad moved to Atlanta three months ago.

My mom was sitting on a dining room chair dressed in jeans, her thin legs propped up on the table. People always think she's too young to be my mother, since my parents had me the week after they graduated from college. I was eight when I put together enough clues to solve the Mystery of the Unplanned Pregnancy. No one plans on being nine months pregnant when they put on a cap and gown. Plus, they got married a few months after I was born, so in my parents' wedding pictures, I'm the one wearing a baby bridesmaid dress. As a result, at every school function involving parents, my mom looks out of place among the suburban, minivan crowd. She's the young, pretty one who is always skidding in ten minutes late, perching awkwardly in the back of the cafeteria or classroom, or picking her way through the rows to a seat my prompt father has saved for her.

"Oh, Alyce, I've gotta go," my mom said into the receiver. "She's home."

The minute she put down the receiver, my mom slapped one hand to her forehead. "Rats! I meant to put the roast in the oven at two o'clock. Don't worry," she called out, disappearing through the swinging door into the kitchen. "It can still be ready by five!"

If we all have spirit animals, then my mom's would be the dingbat. My favorite game as a child was called Help Mommy Find Her ____. Depending on the day, that blank might be filled in with "shoes," "keys," "wallet," "medication," or "movie passes." She created an evacuation plan for all the times we had to fly out of the house suddenly because she forgot about a doctor's appointment or a meeting at school. Racing along in the car, she would enlist my help in concocting a lie. "So, we're going to tell your teacher that there was a family emergency," she might say. "Let's just keep it vague and not offer any details."

Of the hundreds of squabbles I have witnessed between my mom and dad, 90 percent of them started with my mom losing her wallet or forgetting to pay a bill or leaving the garage door open all night.

"Okay, Mom," I yelled back into the kitchen. "I'm going to check email."

I walked down the hall to my bedroom and reminded myself that it was in serious need of a makeover. If you saw my room and had to guess what kind of girl lived there, you would assume she loved My Little Pony and dressed in tulle. My dad painted the walls lavender when I was six, and my mom chose the pink satin-trimmed curtains. I have a tiny desk monopolized by my computer and a bookshelf that's so overcrowded it's barfing books onto the floor. My mom said that if I can keep my room clean for thirty days straight, we'll redecorate. I haven't made it past five.

I logged on and found an email from Dorathea and one from my dad.

I opened Dorathea's first.

Re: question

From: Dorathea Eberhardt (deberhardt@berkeley.edu)

Sent: Fri 9/10 12:12 PM

To: Celia (celia@celiathedark.com)

hey, celia,

to answer your question: yes. if a guy asks you to hang out, it means he likes you AND wants to be your friend. our society is too caught up in defining relationships, like "this person is my friend and that person is my boyfriend." human bonds are more complex than that.

today in my ethics and industry class, we learned that the ivory coast supplies 46 percent of the world's cocoa production and uses child slave labor to farm cocoa fields. the chocolate companies, including the one that monikered your hometown, don't want kids to know about this. you and your friends should stage a protest in

front of the chocolate factory. STOP BIG CHOCOLATE
FROM USING SLAVE LABOR!

how are you adapting to life without the cokehead
around?

dorathea

First off, when Dorathea suggested that me and "my
friends" go stage a protest, I think she forgot about the
email where I mentioned that I was a little low on friends.
Dorathea is politically active. She grew up on the West
Coast, which she says is more "conscious" than Pennsylvania.

Second, my dad's not a cokehead. We call him that
because he went to Atlanta to work for the Coca-Cola
Company. Since he has worked for both Hershey and
Coke, Dorathea also calls him a "corporate tool" or "sugar
pusher." He got his first job at the Hershey Corporation
right after college and started climbing the corporate rope,
knot by knot. When he lost his job at Hershey last year to
downsizing, he said he had to move to Atlanta to work for
Coke because distribution management for international
companies is specialized work.

I opened the email from my dad.

Re: Hello, Celia
From: James Door (jdoor@cocacolacompany.com)
Sent: Fri 9/10 9:39 AM

To: Celia (celia@celiathedark.com)

Hi, Turtle,

Things are great in Atlanta. The new job is flexible, so I run every morning and come to work at ten.

I found three parks within walking distance from my condo and a new shopping mall with lots of teen stores. I'm not far from the library. Can't wait to show you around at Christmas.

Please remind your mother about the mortgage payment.

I Love You,

Dad

My dad's pet name for me is Turtle, or Turtledove. When I was three, Dad sang "The Twelve Days of Christmas" to me at bedtime, adding one more verse each night leading up to Christmas. I was learning my animals, and my dad explained that the "two turtledoves" in the song were birds. After that, I called all flying animals "turtles," and my parents thought it was so cute, a nickname was born.

My parent's informal custody agreement looks like this: Dad gets me for Christmas, summer, and spring break; Mom gets me the rest of the time, and I get no say in the matter. And every Friday, like clockwork, my dad sends me an email. There is a standard template to these communications. They contain at least three things that I would like about Atlanta and end with the same request, "Please remind your mother . . ."

My parents didn't always squabble about Mom's forgetfulness. The first time I remember them fighting was when I was six years old and into a series of books called Jane and Clementine. They were about two sisters who go on wild adventures together, and as a result, I was obsessed by the idea of having a little sister. I asked about it constantly, begging both of my parents to have a baby. The conversations I had with Mom and Dad were very different.

Dad: "Maybe, Turtle, if we're lucky." Then he would smile and pat my leg.

Mom: "You're handful enough for me!" Then she would laugh and kiss me.

One night, after I asked my dad for a baby sister for the twentieth time during my bedtime reading, I overheard my parents talking in their bedroom.

"I always told you that I want a family," said Dad.

"Yes, a family," my mom said back. "We are a *family* of three."

"You have to compromise in a marriage."

"Compromise! Into nine months of pregnancy and the constant work of another child? I want to accomplish things with my life."

"Gina, are you telling me we're twenty-seven and that's it, we're finished having kids?"

"Don't wake Celia."

That was the first time I cried without running into my parents' room for comfort. I lay in bed that night worrying that we might not be a family if we were only a family of three. The next night, I did not ask my father for a baby sister when he read to me at bedtime.

When I was in fifth grade, my mom went back to school for nursing. That was the year she started becoming forgetful.

"Gina, why are we getting a late notice on our water bill?" my dad would bellow after putting down his briefcase and flipping through the mail after work.

"We are both responsible for the bills now, not just me!" my mom would yell back from her desk in their bedroom.

My dad would then mumble something that ended in the phrase "can't live like this," before heading into the kitchen to make dinner.

My mom got her internship at the hospital when I was starting eighth grade, and her work schedule got crazy. She started on the night shift five days a week, so she would be getting home from work in the morning when my dad was leaving. The fighting got worse, and it wasn't just in their room at night.

"Gina, are you taking Celia to the dentist after school?" my dad might ask in the morning as he and I were getting up. My mom, sleepy eyed and preparing for bed, would slap her forehead and say, "Oh no. I forgot. I'm so exhausted. Can we reschedule?"

"Damn it. How much longer are these night shifts going to last?"

"Someone has to work them."

"You have a family."

"We knew there would be sacrifices."

"So we'll add Celia's teeth to the list of sacrifices? Fine, I'll leave work early and take her."

Then one Saturday in April of eighth grade, my mom and dad asked me to come into the living room. It was two weeks after Ruth had been dragged from school, her unbraided hair swinging behind her. I had been in my room rereading *Charlotte's Web*, and as soon as they called me in, I knew something was wrong. They were both sitting up very straight on the sofa, and there was no radio or television playing.

"Celia." My dad cleared his throat; he didn't call me "Turtle." "I've gotten a job offer with another company that would mean greater security for the family."

My mom sat next to him, looking down into her hands. She could have had an invisible book the way she was reading her own palms. She sank deeper into the couch every minute.

"There is a downside to the deal," said my dad. He looked up and met my stare. "The job is in Atlanta."

"Are we moving?" I asked, almost interrupting him. Mentally, I started packing my suitcase. Without Ruth, I had no reason to stay in Hershey.

My dad sighed. "No, Turtle, you and your mom are going to stay here for the present."

I looked back and forth between them like they were a tennis match. I couldn't figure out what my dad was saying.

"Are you leaving us?" I asked without actually believing it was possible.

"You know your mom finally got on to the regular staff at the hospital, and we think it's better for you to stay in the house and have the school environment you're used to . . ." I was having trouble concentrating on my dad's speech because of the panic rushing into my brain, but I distinctly heard the soliloquy end with "trial separation." Sometimes words can have the force of baseball bats.

"Divorce? Are you getting a divorce?"

My mom finally animated. "Your father and I need some time to sort things out, Celia. We haven't decided on a divorce."

"But we don't want you to worry about that," my father added quickly. "We want you to let us worry about the details. We'll still be a family, Turtle," my dad started to choke on the words, "no matter what happens."

"Don't worry about the *details*? Like who I'm going to

live with?" Anxiety started its little fire in my stomach.

"This is what we think is best," my dad said. My mom came over to the chair where I was sitting and tried to put her arm around me.

No was all I managed to say as I wrenched myself from under my mother's arm and bounded down to my room. It was hard to go back to reading *Charlotte's Web* with the tears streaming down my face, but somehow I managed.

x x x

I decided to respond to Dorathea's email before my dad's.

Re: Friendship

From: Celia (celia@celiathedark.com)

Sent: Fri 9/10 3:46 PM

To: Dorathea Eberhardt (deberhardt@berkeley.edu)

hey, Dorathea,

   things are okay without dad, i guess. how long do people have trial separations? if dad likes his job in atlanta, and mom likes her job here, then where are we going to live if they get back together?

   do you know anyone who is gay?

celia

"Celia, come out and be social," my mom called from the kitchen, tearing me away from my email.

I reluctantly logged off and dragged my feet down the hall. The pot roast still had hours to cook, but my mom handed me a potato and a peeler and suggested we have some "girl time." I resisted the urge to tell her that she hadn't been a girl in over a decade.

"So, June Bug," she started, fixing an apron around her neck in an obvious effort to appear domestic. I hadn't seen my mom put on an apron and cook a meal in months. She looked thinner since my dad left. "Tell me about your first week of high school."

It is moments like these that make me want to fling potato peels at my mother's head and scream, "Why did you force me to stay here?" But since all the screaming I did through the months of May and June didn't make a dent in her resolve, I have to settle for being sullen instead.

"It was fine," I answered, blinding my potato with the cone-shaped blade of the peeler.

"What is your favorite class so far?" she prodded, opening the oven to check on her still-pink pot roast and shaking her head slightly.

"I don't know . . . Earth Science, I guess." I remembered Drake turning around to look at me in that class after he was jarred awake by Mr. Diaz yelling, "That's right, inert gases!" Tireless note passer and classroom complainer Debra Madison had actually gotten a question right.

"Science?" said my mother closing the oven door. "But you've always been an English and history girl."

"People change, Mom. Try not to get all worked up."

My mom wiped her hands on her apron even though they obviously weren't wet from looking in the oven. She took a deep breath. I never would have spoken to my mom this way while my dad was still here. But they were the ones who decided to change things, so they should have expected that I would change, too.

"Well, have you made any new friends yet?" she asked brightly, turning back to a new cookbook she bought after my dad left and flipping a few pages.

My mom had no idea I was hanging out with Drake after school because she worked the swing shift so much. It would probably make her happy to hear I had a new friend, even a temporary one. It might make her think she had made the right choice by forcing me to stay in Hershey. I wasn't willing to give her that satisfaction. I just shrugged. "Okay, I'm done peeling potatoes, is that all you wanted?"

"Now you need to cut them into one-inch squares for boiling." She handed me a cutting board. I slapped it down on the counter and started a sloppy job of slicing.

"What book are you reading?" The investigation continued.

"*To Kill a Mockingbird*," I mumbled, wishing I could be in my room reading it. "Dad told me to remind you about the mortgage payment."

My mom sighed again and thumped her hand down on

the cookbook where she was looking at the recipe for Old-Fashioned Pot Roast.

"I told him not to bother you about the bills," she snapped. "Your father can call me if he thinks I need reminders about my responsibilities." She twisted a finger into her curly, brown hair and then pulled it out.

I stopped slicing and stared at her.

"Sorry, Celia." She sighed. "I shouldn't take it out on you. I'll be right back." She took off her apron and headed toward the bathroom.

I finished cutting the potatoes and dropped them into a pot of boiling water on the stove. As tiny bits of the water splashed out, they made hissing noises against the burners. The yellow cubes were tumbling around in the water when the phone rang. I was just going to let it ring, since no one ever called for me, when it occurred to me that it might be Drake. Maybe he was calling on the way to New York for a last-minute check-in before seeing Japhy.

"Hello," I answered, careful not to seem too eager.

"Gina?" asked a man's voice I didn't recognize.

"No."

"Oh, sorry, may I speak with Gina?"

I hesitated, not sure I wanted to let this man, who called my mother by her first name, speak to her. "Gina, there's a man on the phone for you," I yelled down the hall without covering the mouthpiece.

My mother came out of the bathroom carrying a tissue

in one hand and combing her fingers through her hair with the other. She took the receiver from me and put her hand over the end you talk into. "You still call me *Mom*, not Gina," she said before taking away her palm and speaking a sunny hello into the phone.

After a pause, she said, "Oh yes, Simon from the hospital." My mom turned her back to me and twirled the phone cord around her finger. "Sure, that sounds great," she said after another pause. "I'll see you then." She hung up the phone.

"Tell me that wasn't a date," I said with my hands folded over my chest.

My mother looked momentarily startled by my tone. "No," she said defensively, "it wasn't."

"You said it was a *trial* separation. You said you were trying to work things out."

She turned away from the phone and raised her voice. "I am your mother, and you don't get to interrogate me, Celia."

When I stomped down the hall and slammed the door to my room, she didn't try to follow me. I plopped down and opened my email again, even though I knew there wouldn't be anything new. I tried to read, but ended up writing a poem.

Autumn stomps around outside the house
like an annoying little sister, tapping

on all the shutters, kicking up the piles
of leaves you rake, pretending to howl
like a wolf. But I'm glad she's here,
so we can cuss at Summer together,
pretend we don't even remember her name.

My mom didn't bother me again until hours later when she knocked on the door gently and said, "The pot roast is ready."

CHAPTER

12

I'm kind of a public-library celebrity. Between third and eighth grade, I collected the first-place prize for every Summer Reading Star contest in my age group. The librarians got suspicious. After I read *The Catcher in the Rye* at age ten, one looked over her glasses at me and said, "Dear, what was your favorite part of this book?" She acted like she was being sweet and curious, but I knew she thought I was too young to read Salinger.

"I resonated with the way the main character Holden Caulfield is always calling people out on being phony." I said the word *phony* with emphasis. I guess I was a little Dark even before I turned fourteen.

If I was suddenly struck blind, I would still have a pretty good chance of finding my way to the teen section of the library without the use of a guide dog. "Hi, Celia," two different librarians called out before I made it up the stairs and into the back room marked YOUNG ADULT. My mom had a rare Saturday off, so I knew that if I stayed home, I would end up cleaning out the attic or rearranging the silverware drawer. I invented a school project excuse and rode my bike to the Hershey Public Library, which is located, no joke, on Cocoa Avenue.

I relaxed more with each row of books I passed. Then I plopped down on one of the orange plastic sofas intended to make teens comfortable and opened my backpack. I always have my poetry notebook with me. You never know when you will have a few minutes to write, or when you might need distraction or a hiding place.

I've been working for a while on a list of instructions for writing poetry. This seemed like a good opportunity to add some more thoughts.

HOW TO WRITE POETRY
By Celia the Dark

1. *Use your own words. Don't use words like "'tis" or "thou" or "forthwith." It sounds too much like the Bible or Shakespeare.*
2. *Don't rhyme unless you have to because everyone tries to rhyme when they start writing poetry and it makes you sound like everyone else.*
3. *Be specific. Sometimes people are vague in their poems because they think it makes them sound deep.*
4. *If you don't know how to end your poem, just take*

the first two lines from the beginning of your poem
and write them over again at the end. It gives your
poem something called "closure."
5. *Don't be afraid to be Dark.*

I was working on the list, letting the spell of the library hypnotize me, forgetting my anxiety over seeing Drake talking to Sandy, my dull ache for revenge against her, and my mom's call from Simon, when I heard a familiar voice say, "Please . . . just for a minute."

I looked over toward the staircase in time to catch the sight of two heads, each with a blonde braid, disappearing quickly down the stairs. I stood up and followed them to the landing, but the glass door was swinging shut as if someone had just pushed through it. I hurried back, past the couch and over to the nearest window. Below me in the parking lot, I saw a familiar station wagon. Before getting into it, Ruth looked up at me and waved.

At two o'clock on Sunday afternoon, the phone in the kitchen rang. I had spent the morning on odious homework activities and overdue laundry chores. My mom and I had just finished lunch.

"Hello."

"Can you come over?" Drake asked.

"You're home! I didn't think you would be back until tonight." My heart did a Rockettes line of high kicks.

"Are you free? Can you come over now?"

I looked at my mom who was sponging off the table. "Ten minutes," I said.

"Meet me in the lot."

"Gotta go," I said to my mom as I replaced the receiver.

"Where?" she asked, pulling crumbs from the table into her hand.

"To . . . see . . . a friend," I managed, although I knew it would unleash a pack of question-sniffing dogs.

"Does this friend have a name, address, and social security number?" Parents are so predictably nosy.

"Drake," I mumbled, pulling my sneakers out of the hall closet. "Cloverdale Avenue."

"Oh, a *boy*," she said, dumping her palm crumbs into the trash.

"Yes, Mom, a friend with male genitalia. Leaving now," I said, grabbing my backpack from its spot near the door and backing out.

"Remember I'm on night shift tonight," she said as I pulled the door closed, "and they're calling for rain today."

When I reached Drake's house, I walked across the neatly kept grass, past the flower beds, and into the thick blanket of leaves in the wooded lot. Fall was evident in the canopy. Every day the trees showed more of their naked limbs.

As I made my way in, I could see Drake already sitting on our regular log. He was holding his skateboard upside down between his knees and prying at something.

"What are you doing?" I asked, dropping my backpack into a mound of tree roots.

"Trying to pop a rusty bearing out of this wheel," he said. "Got a new one this weekend."

I took a Sharpie out of my hoodie pocket and propped my low tops up on the nurse log. I started drawing shapes on the white toes.

"How did it go?"

"Not so good."

I examined Drake's face. His jaw muscles were fixed,

like he was grinding his teeth together. He was working on his skateboard with the intensity of a surgeon. I blacked out the word *Converse* on my shoe with a five-point star.

"I got so nervous waiting for Saturday night," Drake said through his tight jaw. "Friday at the show and all day Saturday, I felt like my body was trying to eat itself from the inside out. I kept pacing around the apartment or making excuses to go outside. When Japhy finally rang the doorbell, my hands were shaking as I opened it." Drake's screwdriver slipped and made a scraping sound against the bottom of his board. "Shit."

I stopped drawing on my shoe and looked at Drake. I put the cap on the Sharpie.

"My mom left for the show with his dad since Japhy's mom and my dad were already at the theatre. The minute they were gone, Japhy took off his sweater and said, 'Let's drink some of your dad's whiskey.' I'd never had alcohol before. I don't think he had either." Drake kept working the screwdriver into the wheel as he spoke. He wasn't looking at me, like he was telling the story to his skateboard.

"I felt so panicked about talking to him. I thought, *Maybe I should have a drink. Maybe this will be easier.* So we opened the liquor cabinet, and he waved around the bottle and said, 'Look, Drake . . . the envelope.' I mixed my whiskey with Coke, but Japhy just poured his over some ice. Then we climbed onto the fire escape to people watch. I didn't feel much. At least, I didn't feel *drunk* the way people describe it. I did feel a little more relaxed. We decided to have another one."

The wind started to shuffle the leaves around our feet. It was always cooler in the wooded lot than out on the grassy lawns of the neighborhood. I pulled on my hood.

"Japhy turned the music up loud and made our second drinks with vodka. This time he mixed mine with less Coke and didn't put any ice in his at all. We went back out on the fire escape and called things to the people down on the street. Japhy would yell, 'Hey, dude, you dropped something,' and then keep directing the person to some imaginary object like, 'Right behind you . . . a little to the left . . . there, don't you see it?' until the guy figured out that he was messing with him. He did it to three different people before—" Suddenly, the screwdriver slipped again and tore a thin line of blood across the top of Drake's left hand. "Damn it!" He threw the screwdriver into the leaves like it was a snake that had bitten him.

"Are you okay?" I sat up on the log. "Let me see it."

Drake shook his head and tucked his injured hand under his other arm, squeezing it to his torso without showing it to me. "Fire escapes are tiny, so we had to sit close together and press against each other every time we wanted to move. After he tricked the third guy on the sidewalk, he was laughing and he looked at me. His face was close to mine and he looked so happy and I just . . . kissed him. I kissed him."

The wind picked up a pile of leaves and dumped them on Drake's feet. His hair blew into his eyes despite the styling product. "And?" I held my breath.

"He kissed me back." Drake pulled his injured hand out and looked at the red line across his skin where a few droplets of blood were forming. "And it was amazing. Everything in New York went silent. The fire escape detached from the building and flew around the city like a helicopter. The sun went down and came up again. It was perfect." Drake ran his good hand through his hair. I exhaled, imagining two boys kissing on a fire escape in the sky. "Until he pushed me away and said 'I gotta go.' Then he pushed me again, even though we weren't touching anymore."

Drake started pacing through the leaves. The wind was picking up strength each minute, and it felt like a storm was coming. It started getting dark even though it was late afternoon.

"What happened?" I asked, rooting in my backpack now for Band-Aids.

"He climbed through the window and back into the apartment; I followed him. And I was so close to telling him. I mean, I was seconds away from telling him everything I was feeling, when he said, 'I'm not gay,' and he grabbed his stuff and ran out the door. He actually *ran*."

I felt helpless. I looked desperately until I found a tiny first aid kit hiding out in the bottom of my bag. Part of having a nurse for a mom. I motioned for Drake to sit down next to me, and carefully took hold of his injured hand. I tore open the wrapper, pulled off the slick paper and covered Drake's cut.

"I went back to the fire escape and watched him run all the way down the street toward the subway. I cried. I thought about jumping off. I thought about drinking all the whiskey and the vodka," Drake said. "But I ended up just putting the bottles away and going to bed. My mom came in my room when she got home and asked if Japhy and I had a fight because he had texted his parents to tell them he went home. They were all angry because Japhy left and took the subway alone at night. That's funny, huh?" said Drake, even though it wasn't funny.

"I told my parents I wanted to take the train back early today. I didn't tell them what really happened with Japhy, I just said I needed to get back and do some homework," he finished, stuffing his bandaged hand into his jacket pocket. "I feel so stupid. I'm so stupid."

A few fat raindrops plopped onto my shoulder, and the wind picked up more leaves and dumped them against our log.

"So much for coming out," Drake said, kicking at the leaves that were trying to bury us. "Being in the closet isn't so bad. Closets are warm and cozy, and filled with clothes," he said without smiling.

My heart cracked right down the middle. I couldn't think of one useful thing to say.

Drake stood up to fish around for his screwdriver in the leaves where he threw it. I picked up his skateboard as five more heavy drops fell on my back.

Then we turned and put our arms around each other. The sky opened its mouth and cried all over us.

"We'll have to remove the hand," I said, inspecting Drake's cut Monday morning on the way to school.

"What about my career as a circus knife-thrower?" He stepped on his skateboard.

"We can get you transferred to the sideshow freak department."

Drake slid down the sidewalk beside me listlessly, barely spending the effort to push. Luckily, the path to school was mostly downhill.

"Are you okay?" I ventured.

"Well, I'm dying. We're all dying, and everything we do on Earth is pointless, but yeah," said Drake without passion. "I'm fine."

At school, we parted ways to go to our lockers, and Drake rode his skateboard down the hall, which is massively illegal at Hershey High. I watched him stop and flip his board up into his hand just as Mr. Foster, our principal, stepped out of the nurse's office. Principal Foster looked at Drake, nodded, and kept walking.

Becky Shapiro, who has the locker next to mine, was dialing her combination when I arrived. If Becky was just overweight at the start of eighth grade, she was obese by the beginning of ninth.

"Hey, Celia," she said kindly. Becky has a small crew of friends, gamer girls mostly. They might have accepted me into their group in eighth grade if I had tried. I guess I didn't try.

"Hey, Becky," I said back, opening my locker. My CELIA THE DARK sign had disappeared over the weekend. It could have been a janitor. We're technically only allowed to decorate the inside of our lockers.

"Do you want to buy a candy bar to support the band?" Becky asked, pulling a box of Hershey's chocolate bars out of her locker.

Hershey Corp. gives chocolate bars to local schools to raise money for things like cheerleading camps and musicals. So, at any given time, half of the kids in Hershey are selling candy bars and the other half are buying them. I refuse to eat Hershey's chocolate because I refuse to be a cog in the great American corporate machine. I was about to tell Becky that when Joey Gaskill walked down the hall, flanked by two of his meatheads. "A fat girl selling candy bars *always* makes me hungry!" The guys with Joey started laughing, big dumb laughs falling out of their mouths like drool.

I felt the Darkness rise up in my chest. Before I could

stop myself, I slammed my locker and turned around. "You're stupid and mean, and you suck at basketball."

Danger filled the hallway. Joey stopped short and shined his menace on me like a spotlight. I braced for direct, physical violence.

"The troll speaks," he said, looking me up and down. "It's okay, I'm not trying to steal your fat girlfriend."

"Keep marching, hate parade," I said in a Dark voice, pointing down the hall.

"Such a weird little gremlin," he said back, shaking his head and backing down the hall with his minions. His voice was casual, but his look was murderous.

My heart was pumping enough blood for three bodies. I felt my skin hardening into armor as I turned to open my locker again. Becky was staring at her box of candy bars, her chest bowed in like she had been punched in the stomach. Tears stood at the corner of her eyes ready to jump to their death on her cheeks. "Thanks, Celia," she whispered. I just nodded.

People criticize kids for being fat, but then hand us birthday cake and Valentine's chocolate, Saint Patrick's Day cupcakes, and everything at Christmas. Looking at Becky, you know that she isn't just fat because she likes to eat cookies. She's using the fat for something, like punishment or protection. I think Becky is fat for the same reason I'm Dark.

My hands were still shaking when I got to first period. I was doing everything I could to control my breathing as Mr. Pearson walked around the room returning the assignments we turned in on Friday—essays on the poem "We Real Cool" by Gwendolyn Brooks. I had decided to write my paper in the form of a poem.

In Gwendolyn Brooks' poem "We Real Cool," what poetic devices does the poet use to convey meaning? Does Gwendolyn Brooks think it is cool to leave school?

DYING IS NOT HOT
By Celia the Dark

Cool is no longer cool because cool is now hot,
and school isn't school if you're skipping.
Then the neighborhood is school and John,
the creepy dropout guy is teaching.

And it isn't cool because the cool kids stay in school,
where the other cool kids tell them how hot they are
and they wouldn't want to miss a dance for cutting.

Kids who skip school were never cool or hot but
already dumped into the trashcan with leftover lunch pizza,

bruised into a locker, asking their parents for extra lunch
   money
so they can smoke and act like they never cared anyway.

And skipping's not cool but it is school
because that's where they learn what the un-cool learn
about life and dying.

I even ended the poem with death the way Gwendolyn Brooks ended her poem. Plus, I said way more about
what it's like to skip school now. I mean, does anyone play
hooky to go to a pool hall? Either kids really did that in,
like, 1960 or she just said that because it rhymed.

When he handed my work back, balding Mr. Pearson,
who looks like he's never been inspired by a poem in his
life, said, "Celia, what is this? I said write an *essay*. Do it
over." Mandy laughed quietly to herself.

A whole tree splintered inside me, just like it had been
struck by lightning. My mouth opened and said, "Shut the
fuck up, Amanda," while my leg reached over to kick her
desk so hard that it moved a foot.

Language Arts exploded. "What did you say?" Mandy
jumped out of her chair. Sandy spun around like she had
never heard such language. Mr. Pearson put up his hands
like a referee and metaphorically blew a whistle. "Mandy,
sit down. Celia, detention, tomorrow." He pointed a beefy
finger right in my face. Mandy flipped her long hair over

one shoulder and made a show of pushing her chair back into place and sitting down again.

"I don't tolerate that language or that behavior in my class, Ms. Door," Mr. Pearson said as he walked to his desk and dramatically pulled a detention form out of his drawer. I felt sick enough to vomit down the back of Sandy's sweater. My bones were full of dry ice and my ears were smoking. I couldn't believe I just lost my mind like that. *English? I just got detention in English?* English was supposed to be my safe harbor, my happy place. I closed my eyes and tried to remember Ms. Green's class. This never would have happened with Ms. Green.

Ms. Green was my eighth-grade English teacher. In her class, I never got below an A. She was the first person to suggest that I write a poem. She did a lot more for me, too.

She always wore high heels and pencil skirts, while the other teachers wore shapeless dresses and clogs or flats. She had brown hair that swung around her shoulders like she was in a shampoo commercial. Ms. Green didn't miss one day of school when I was in eighth grade. She was never sick or on vacation. No one in her family died. She was the only teacher who never had a substitute, and at the end of the year, the principal gave her a plaque to acknowledge her lack of absences.

All the desks in Ms. Green's classroom were arranged in a circle surrounding a braided rug with an overstuffed armchair and reading lamp. Every Friday, Ms. Green turned out the fluorescent lights and let sunlight flicker through the blinds while she read poems out loud. Once, she cried while reading us a poem about a girl whose father had died. She didn't stop reading the poem, she just kept reading through her tears. It wasn't just the boys in my class who swooned over Ms. Green. I think the entire eighth grade was in love with her.

It was May, a month after Ruth's mother took her out of school and two weeks after my parents announced their trial separation, when Ms. Green handed me the note. She was walking around the circle in front of our desks and handing back our papers on the book *Night* by Elie Wiesel. She stopped at each desk, resting one high heel against the other as she put down a paper in front of each student.

The papers were identical, all stapled at the top, left corner with a letter grade and her red handwriting above the title. When she stopped at my desk, she paused for a second. I looked up at her as her hair fell around her face like a hood and she smiled her straight-teeth smile. She put down a paper with a purple sticky note affixed to the front and then, without speaking, she continued around the room. The note said:

Celia,
You have talent as a writer. In my eight years of teaching,
I haven't come across a more natural and engaging voice.
I hope that you will continue to work hard and hone your

craft both in school and in your spare time. I believe you
have been given a gift.
Ms. Green

A tingly feeling started at the base of my skull. It crept
all the way around my head and stretched my mouth into
a smile. Ms. Green had noticed me! Ms. Green thought I
had a gift! I sat staring at the purple note until I got the
prickly feeling that another set of eyes had joined mine on
the paper. I glanced to my left just in time to see Sandy
Firestone, seated next to me, with her eyes glued to Ms.
Green's note.

As soon as she felt my gaze on her, Sandy's eyes darted
around the floor as if she was innocently looking for a
dropped pencil. I glanced at Sandy's paper and noticed a
large, red C sitting there like a mouth hanging open.

Sandy looked up and saw my eyes on her paper. She
snatched it up and shoved it into her notebook, slamming
the cover closed.

That's the day the trouble started. The trouble that
nearly ruined my life. The trouble that turned me Dark.
The trouble that begs me for revenge.

FORM OF REVENGE	PRO	CON
Trip her in the hall	Embarrassing but not public enough	Not clever, involves physical violence, could get suspended
Post a photo of her online with mean caption	Mildly embarrassing	Have to find photo, would enough people see it?
Steal one of her bad English papers and spread it around	Might be able to steal it in L.A.	Being bad at school is not very embarrassing

I spent the rest of L.A. working on a Revenge Plan Pro & Con list. Since I want my revenge to cause humiliation and be public, and for Sandy to know that I orchestrated it, it wasn't the easiest plan to concoct. Also, I wasn't thinking clearly because my heart was beating so fast. By the end of class, I had gotten nowhere. As everyone was standing up and shuffling out of the room, Mandy kicked my chair subtly and whispered, "Watch out, Weird."

Before lunch, I waited for Drake at my locker while he

dropped off his science book. He was walking down the hall toward me when I witnessed a scene. A group of girls was standing around another bank of freshman lockers when Drake tried to walk by. One girl pushed another girl hard on the back so she fell right into him, dropping the book she was holding. Drake looked surprised at first, but then he gave the girl a charming smile and picked up her book. When he walked away, the girls exploded into giggles like they were toy volcanoes that erupt in pink icing.

"Hey," said Drake flatly when he reached my locker.

Over his shoulder, I could see that the girls were still watching him, transfixed by our interaction. Drake seemed unaware of the audience.

"Hey," I said back, closing my locker and walking with Drake away from the girls and toward the doors to the picnic area. I glanced back over my shoulder once to find that they were still staring.

A brooding quiet joined us for lunch on the lawn that day. We both chewed our sandwiches with lazy mouths like horses gnawing on grass.

"Not playing the pickup game?" I asked, noticing the basketball players collecting on the court while Drake sat unmoving.

"Not feeling it," he mumbled, and went back to chewing.

"I got detention," I said.

"Of course you did"—he chewed—"because everything sucks today." When he said the word *sucks*, a little piece of tuna sandwich projected out of his mouth and landed on my hoodie sleeve. It flew right through the tension and forced us both to laugh. Drake took a napkin and wiped it off for me.

"Do you want to buy tickets to the homecoming dance?" a high-pitched voice piped. I looked over and saw a girl in jeans and a Hershey High sweatshirt bouncing over to us from the picnic tables. She was trailed by another girl holding a metal cash box, and they both had paint on their faces that said *Junior* on one cheek and *Class* on the other. "It's on October second," she said.

"No thanks," Drake answered politely. I just shook my head, sending the spirited juniors on to the next group of students sitting in the grass.

"Will you still be here on October second?" I asked, trying not to sound too invested in Drake's departure date.

"Who knows? My parents called both admissions offices, but I'm still on the wait list. It's not like I have much to go back for now anyway. Then again, it's not like I have much to stay here for." He put his head on his hands and lay back in the grass as the other boys started the pickup game.

I put the rest of my sandwich into my bag, having fully lost my appetite.

"Back again, Celia?" Ms. Edgar, the school librarian, greeted Drake and me warmly when we drew open the double doors to our library. I had asked Drake to walk to school early on Tuesday so I could exchange my book. I still hadn't returned *Foreignisms*, so I felt I was getting behind on my Dewey decimal project. Also, I wanted a new book to read during detention.

Detention. It was the first word that came to my mind when I woke up that day. I couldn't imagine what horrors awaited me there. Luckily, Mom was working the swing shift again, so I didn't have to mention it to her over dinner Monday night. Plus, she wasn't telling me anything about Simon from the hospital, so I didn't feel the need to tell her about detention. You could get two of them before a letter went home requesting a conference with your parent.

"Morning," I said back to Ms. Edgar, trying not to sound too Dark. I was wearing a short, black skirt and my thick-soled combat boots again, along with some purple striped tights. My boots and hoodie were turning into my school uniform.

Drake looked sleepy, and his hair wasn't styled. He hardly talked on the walk to school. But as soon as we walked into the library, he whispered, "I tried texting him last night. I emailed, too. He un-friended me online." Drake didn't have to tell me who *he* was. There was a deep well of sadness in Drake's eyes.

We walked along the nonfiction books, closest to the glass doors. The next section after language was science, the 500 class. I browsed through titles on planets, the nuclear age, and biodomes, looking for the next topic to grab my interest.

"Maybe he will . . . change his mind?" I said, but didn't sound convincing.

"Yeah," said Drake, but didn't sound hopeful.

Drake took a left turn and headed off into the stacks. I finally chose a book called *The Kingdom of the Earthworm* from the gardening section and went to the circulation desk to check it out.

Drake was tucked into an aisle on the other side of the room, 100–199, philosophy and psychology. He was squatting down on his heels and reading through spines. As I waited for Ms. Edgar to scan my barcode, he approached the desk with one fat book wrapped in a shiny red-and-white dust jacket. The book Drake tossed onto the circulation desk was called *Dream It! Do It!* by Buddy Strong.

✘ ✘ ✘

My pink slip was delivered to Language Arts, providing me with directions to detention. Whenever these little pink wrist-slaps get delivered to class, kids make "oohing" sounds and turn to stare at the person getting one. When Sandy Firestone eyeballed me getting my pink slip, she said in a voice miraculously loud enough for every kid to hear yet inaudible to the teacher, "Detention just got weirder!" The laughter that rippled through the room made my blood thick.

✘ ✘ ✘

In fifth grade, all of our teachers said the same thing. "You kids are going to middle school next year. This kind of laziness isn't going to fly in the sixth grade." It was the same thing in grade eight. "You know, you kids aren't going to get away with this kind of sloppy work in high school. Not in high school, you're not."

I worried about high school so much that when I was still in eighth grade, I bought a copy of the Hershey High yearbook to prepare. The name of the yearbook is—you guessed it—*The Chocolatier*. For a freshman entering high school, the yearbook is like a catalog of cliques. You can browse through the pages and imagine your life in a series of social groups. I tried to imagine myself with the theatre kids or the debate club, but I couldn't picture it. Before I even entered high school, I felt doomed to be one of the kids confined to the posed photographs, never to be featured in a candid.

I got out my notebook and added a few more revenge ideas while Mr. Pearson rambled on about the challenges of writing in dialect.

FORM OF REVENGE	PRO	CON
Pour itching powder down the back of her shirt in L.A.	Irritating and potentially painful	Need a major diversion to avoid getting noticed, and not truly humiliating
Slip melting chocolate bars into her coat pockets	Fantastically gross	Probably get caught and not embarrassing

The rest of morning classes fused into one another as the hours counted down to the last bell. In the hall on our way to lunch, Drake pretended to be onstage.

"Thank you so much for coming to hear me read tonight at Carnegie Hall," Drake was saying in a mock falsetto. "My new book of poems is entitled *Pink Slip* and was inspired by my experiences at a repressive public school in rural Pennsylvania, where I was forced to join the local ruffians in a barbaric confinement called detention—"

"Drake!" said a voice so loud we both jumped. Mr. Scott, Hershey High's basketball coach/gym teacher, approached us. "Drake," he said again in the only volume sports coaches have: loud. "You thinking about next year? You stay on your jump shot, I think you could make varsity as a sophomore. Hey, Cindy, how ya doing?" he added, looking at me.

I looked back at him Darkly.

Coach Scott always watched part of the pickup games at lunch, so he had seen Drake play.

"Hey, Mr. Scott," Drake said back, shrugging. "I'll be back in New York next year. Maybe even next month." Drake didn't sound happy or positive when he said that.

"Well, if you end up staying longer, maybe we can still get you on the team this year," the coach went on. "I might be losing some players." He said that last part behind his hand, as if it was a secret, but he said it just as loudly as everything else. He patted Drake hard on both shoulders and strode off down the hall quickly before Drake could protest.

Drake shook his head at me and said, "Come on, Cindy," and tugged me into Earth Science.

At the end of the day, I said good-bye to Drake and plodded fearfully to the detention hall.

The helpful walking map on my pink slip aided me in moping all the way to the right corridor. STUDY HALL/ DETENTION read the sign on the door. I took a deep breath and opened it.

✗ ✗ ✗

Inside, I found a normal classroom full of desks. A gray-haired man with a pointy chin sitting behind a wooden table took my pink slip and pointed me to a desk in the front row. There were two dejected-looking upperclassmen in the back of the room, slumped in their chairs, their long legs spreading out into the aisles. I sat down and crossed my legs, hoping to seem small and harmless.

A few seconds later, the door opened again, and if I had been chewing gum, I would have swallowed it. In walked Clock, his black trench coat billowing out behind him like a cape. He tossed his pink slip on the gray-haired man's table without looking at him and slid into a desk right next to me as if we had planned on meeting there.

"What's up, Weird? Get detention for macking on your boyfriend in the halls?" he asked with his mouth much too close to my face. His breath smelled like Fritos mixed with toothpaste.

"No way, Mr. Kloch," said the gray-haired man, standing up. "Sunglasses off and seated at this desk." He pointed to a seat two rows away from me.

Clock grabbed the desk he was sitting in with both hands and swung himself into the aisle with a flourish. Then he deposited himself in the appointed desk with the same dramatic flare.

The teacher with the pointy chin rolled his eyes. "Okay, thirty-minute detention starts now. No eating. No talking. No note passing. No cell phones. No gum. No leaving early. No questions. No laptops. No magazines. You may have two books and one notebook out on your desk. Begin."

Clock must have been a regular, because he was mouthing all the words along with the teacher, who either didn't notice or didn't care. The man sat down again at his table and resumed whatever work teachers do when they are forced to stay late at school. The two older boys in the back appeared to be in some state of half sleep or possible coma. They didn't move to get out any books.

Clock started making hand signals at me. He was using two of his fingers to gesture, but I couldn't tell if he was trying to get me to run out of the room with him or if he was indicating some lewd sexual act. Either way, I averted my eyes and tried to ignore him.

I got out my library book and my poetry notebook.

Earthworm *is the common name for the largest members of* Oligochaeta *in the phylum* Annelida. *Earthworms play a major role in converting large pieces of organic matter into rich humus, and thus improving soil fertility.*

I tried to start with page one of my library book, but my mind kept wandering away from the earthworm kingdom. How could I have cursed Mandy out right in front of a teacher? I could practically hear Sandy and Mandy laughing and high-fiving each other for the way they landed me in detention. I let them win *again*. I was allowing my friendship with Drake to distract me from my purpose, my primary reason for showing up to school every day. I needed a plan, a finessed, precise outline for my revenge.

I took out my poetry notebook and continued brainstorming.

FORM OF REVENGE	PRO	CON
Put blue hair color in her shampoo in gym	No lasting physical damage but very public	Might backfire & make her look cool
Spread a rumor that she is dating Clock	VERY embarrassing	Not very believable, probably wouldn't catch on

I wanted my revenge to be full of poetic justice, to counteract what Sandy and Mandy did to me in eighth grade. I wanted the whole school to see Sandy as a pathetic social climber with nothing genuinely cool to offer, but the right plan wasn't clicking. I ended up writing a poem instead.

HERSHEY HIGH AS BODY

The classroom bell like a slow heartbeat
pumps students through the hallways of your veins.

Your cafeteria growls and your doors close
like eyelids at night when you sleep.
What do you dream about, high school?
Do you dream that you are a hospital,
keeping us alive with your textbook-heart monitors,
your basketball court, an emergency room?
When I fall down in the hallway,
my books spraying over the floor like vomit,
you wish you could pull your mortar arms
out of the earth and pick me up.
But you can't help me. No one can.

CHAPTER

17

After detention I walked home alone. *This is what it will be like again after Drake leaves*, I thought. Alone. The house was empty when I opened my front door, and everything was soaked with a thick gravy of quiet. I did my homework, all of it but that essay on "We Real Cool" for Mr. Pearson. I already wrote a poem on the subject, and he should have accepted that. I put it off.

When I approached our walking to school meeting spot on Wednesday morning, I was shocked to find Drake already there, sitting on a swing with a book in his lap. His head was leaning against the metal chain, and his skateboard was sitting in the wood chips beside him.

"Hey," I said, walking up to the swings.

His head jolted from its resting place. "Whoa," he said, looking at me, "I guess I fell asleep."

"Don't you know coffee is the most important meal of the day?"

"Barely slept last night." He started putting his book into his backpack. "Up late reading." I noticed that the book he was holding was the one he checked out from the library, the one with the red-and-white cover.

Drake stood up and yawned, stretching his arms overhead. "My mom says I can't walk to school with you anymore, now that you're a hardened criminal."

"Good thing she's in another state so she never has to know," I said back.

Despite being tired, Drake looked the happiest I had seen him since his trip to New York.

"Did you hear from Japhy yet?" I asked as we started toward school.

"He hasn't returned two emails, five texts, and a phone call," Drake answered, a dark shadow crossing his face. "But I'm feeling more optimistic," he said cryptically. "Come over today?"

"Can't. Mom's day off. She says because she works so much, we need to hang out whenever she's home on a weeknight."

"Tomorrow?"

"Sure."

"There's something I want to talk to you about."

"What?"

"Tell you later."

✕ ✕ ✕

That morning I sat behind Sandy in L.A. stabbing any of her blonde hairs that fell on my desk with a pen. I ignored Mr.

Pearson's lecture on responsible scholarship and continued brainstorming.

FORM OF REVENGE	PRO	CON
Slip drugs into her locker through the vent and tell the principal she's a dealer	Public	Where do you get drugs? Not exactly humiliating
Slip test answers into her notebook and accuse her of cheating	Sort of embarrassing & could get her in trouble	Forces me to be a snitch & where would I get test answers?

It wasn't until the end of the day, when I was waiting for Drake at my locker to walk home, that the calm waters of my Wednesday turned choppy. Drake appeared in the hall with Sandy wrapped around his arm like a boa constrictor. I knew they had second-period Spanish together, but since I had witnessed her whispering to him the week before, I hadn't seen them interact. They were walking slowly down the hall, their feet in sync with one another, their eyes locked.

The black hole started opening in my chest. My mouth tasted like I had just tongue-kissed a battery. I tore my eyes off of them and stared at the math book inside my locker.

"Hey, Hermione," said Drake in a chipper voice. "Trying to decode another evil hex with your book knowledge?"

I turned around. Standing inside the sacred two-foot perimeter around my locker was Drake, locked at the elbow with the sheep-clad wolf herself, Sandy. I couldn't summon my Darkness fast enough. I just stared.

"So, I can't walk home with you today because I have to work on a Spanish project with Sandy," Drake said casually. He dropped his arm to put his hand in one pocket, and Sandy unthreaded her arm from his, looking reluctant.

"Hi, Celia," she said, grinning.

"Whatever, Drake," I said, ignoring Sandy. "It's not like you have to report to me."

Drake's mouth dropped open, but no words came out. Finally, he said, "Oh, yeah. I just wanted . . . you to know. Well, I'll see you later."

They started walking back up the hall in the direction of the front entrance. "Bye, Celia," Sandy called, without turning her head back toward me.

I looked into my locker, praying I had enough Darkness to keep me from crying at school. Squeezing my eyes closed, I tried to slow my heart. I felt a hand on my shoulder.

"Is it cool if I call you later?" Drake asked. "There's something I really want to talk to you about." I turned just enough to see him standing there alone. Sandy was waiting down the hall. He had come back to talk to me.

I shrugged. "Whatever." I did not cry. I kept staring at my math book.

So Drake said, "Okay, I'll call you later," and he ran off down the hall.

CHAPTER

18

When I got home, I waved as I swept past Mom, who was talking on the phone, and went to my room. My heart was threatening to run away from my chest. Sandy was scheming to turn Drake against me, to take away the one thing I had going for me, that part was obvious. But what about Drake?

Was he naïve about the whole thing, innocently agreeing to partner with her in Spanish? People don't generally lock arms with their Spanish partners. Drake would probably only be here a month, but maybe he still wanted cooler friends. Or, maybe now that things were over with Japhy, Drake was thinking about staying and finding a more promising social group. What if he was somewhere with her right now, telling her all about Japhy, coming out to her, bonding with her?

I paced back and forth in the only clean part of my room available for pacing. Three steps and turn, three steps and turn. I grabbed my backpack and snatched my notebook out of it, flopping down on my bed to write. I started scribbling down more forms of revenge, ignoring the pro and con columns.

FORM OF REVENGE
Laxatives in her lunch
Dead cats in her locker
Bucket of paint on her head at the prom

"Celia?" Mom's voice rang down the hall.

"Yeah?" I yelled back.

"Come and help me with dinner."

"I'm busy right now," I yelled.

"You're going to help eat, so you need to help cook."

I slammed my notebook shut and stalked out to the kitchen.

"Stir this gravy while I go turn the sprinkler off in the backyard. I forgot and left it on last night," she said, holding the end of a wooden spoon over a saucepan.

"Big surprise," I mumbled.

"What's that?"

"Nothing."

I took the spoon and stirred fast, tight circles through the thin gravy, splashing some onto the burner, which sizzled. A minute after my mom slid back the screen door and went into the backyard, the phone in the dining room rang. I jumped to get it, leaving the spoon to float in the gravy pan.

"Drake?"

"Um, Hello. Is . . . Gina there?" The voice sounded confused. It was the same man who called before. *Simon.*

I glanced through the window into the backyard and saw my mom turning off the spigot attached to the garden hose. Then I dropped the receiver right back onto the hook. *Nice try, Simon.* I carefully removed the phone again to make sure I was getting a dial tone and then I rested it on one side of its cradle, so it would register as busy. I didn't feel like hearing from Simon, or Drake for that matter. *If he likes Sandy Firestone so much, he can keep her,* I thought Darkly.

I closed the door to the dining room and rescued the gravy just as it started to burn. When my mom came back in through the screen door, I was stirring vigorously.

"Ground's a little soggy, but we avoided a flood," she said, pushing the hair away from her face with the back of her hands. "Did I hear the phone ring?"

"Yeah," stir, stir, stir, "it was," concoct a lie, ". . . my friend, Drake."

"The new friend who's a boy. Should I know more?"

"He's a friend. It's no big deal."

My mom looked at me as she washed her hands in the kitchen sink. "I think friends are always a big deal," she said. Since my mom started seeing her therapist in July, she says lots of dorky things like that.

x x x

After dinner, I told my mom I had homework and went to my room to check email. She must have found the phone off the hook, because I heard her talking in the dining room. I hoped it wasn't Simon telling her I hung up on him. There was nothing new in my in-box, so I was forced to distract myself with math. For over an hour, I lay on my bed with my mind shifting between math homework and revenge.

Had Sandy successfully won over Drake? What is the Pythagorean theorem? Was she ever going to get tired of trying to ruin my life? Draw an isosceles triangle. Would I ever come up with a good plan to ruin hers? How do you determine the diameter of a circle? Finally, I put my head down on my comforter and lost consciousness. I was lying there, still in my clothes on top of my bed, when a tap on my window startled me awake.

I sat up with a gasp and looked over to see a figure standing in our flower bed, looking in through the glass. It was Drake. The clock on my nightstand said 10:32. I rubbed my eyes as I got up from my bed.

"Do you know that murderers stand in flower beds and tap on windows?" I hissed, sliding open the window and talking to Drake through the screen.

"Zombies, too," he answered, propping his forearms on the sill. "I called your phone two thousand times. Ever heard of call-waiting?"

"Mom doesn't answer it," I said, neglecting to mention the time the phone spent off the hook.

I looked at him standing carefully with one foot on either side of my mom's chrysanthemums. I was feeling guarded because Drake had been with Sandy, talking about who knows what, but I was also excited to see him. I moved the screen, reached a hand through the window and helped him climb in.

"I didn't want to knock this late because of your mom," Drake said, flopping down on my bed once he was inside, "and I couldn't wait until tomorrow."

"Couldn't wait?" Maybe he couldn't wait to tell me that he made a new best friend named Sandy Firestone.

"I couldn't wait to tell you about . . . this," he said, reaching into his backpack and pulling out the red-and-white book he checked out of the library.

"You're reading a book?" I asked with a profound lack of interest.

"Not just any book, Celia," said Drake, lighting up like a summer firefly. "This book is life changing."

I walked to the door and put my ear against it to listen for evidence that my mother might still be awake. With her wacky work hours, she didn't have a usual bedtime. I wasn't sure how much trouble I would get into for having a boy in my room this late. No boy had ever knocked on my window before, day or night.

I didn't hear anything, so I walked back over to the bed, where Drake was holding the book. When I sat down, he handed it to me, its title splashed across the cover in metallic blue letters: *Dream It! Do It!* by Buddy Strong.

My mom got into self-help books last summer after my dad left, so I was used to "You can do it!" language, and had became increasingly allergic to the hyper-positivity of the genre. Around my house, I had found it difficult not to roll my eyes whenever I heard the word *intentionality*.

"When I first got back from New York, I was so depressed," Drake said, taking off his sneakers and tossing them into the corner of the room where my shoes were already piled. "I felt like everything was over, like things were hopeless."

"You mean yesterday?" Drake ignored my snarkiness. I turned the book over once and then tossed it onto the bed next to me.

"Yeah." He gestured toward me like I had just made a good point. "Just yesterday I was being so negative and acting so defeated. I really took my eyes off the prize." He crossed his legs and sat facing me. I didn't face him back but sat awkwardly looking toward my computer. "I know this might seem really out there to you, all woo-woo and big city, but promise me you'll be open-minded."

"Do you think we country mice can't get transcendent?" I said to my computer screen.

"What? No. Celia." Drake took my hands and pulled my body around to face his. "I mean that I know this might sound stupid, but I really want to share it with you."

It did soften my heart when Drake said he wanted to share something with me. Maybe the whole Sandy thing was meaningless. Maybe it was nothing but a Spanish project, and I was completely overreacting.

"This book is . . . I don't know, it's just, speaking to me," Drake said, picking it up off the bed and turning it over a few times in his hands. "It's like . . . it isn't telling me anything I don't know, but it's saying it in a way that I can really *hear* it. Just listen to the introduction. Then you can decide if you want to do the exercises with me. Just promise me you will keep an open mind, okay?"

"Drake, I need to ask you something—" I couldn't contain my curiosity about his time with Sandy any longer.

"I know, I know you have questions, but just let me read the introduction to you first. Please?"

"But there is something I need to know—"

"Just the introduction, that's all I ask."

Reluctantly, I adjusted myself to sit cross-legged across from him on the bed. Drake pulled open the cover on the book like he was opening a pharaoh's tomb. I closed my eyes and tried to let my mind open, or whatever.

"Introduction: The Dream Is the Means and the End

"Too many of us spend our lives reacting to the circumstances and conditions life hands us, thinking the scope of our accomplishments is made possible by our external situation. Hi, I'm Buddy Strong, and in this book, Dream It! Do It!, I'll show you how you can make your greatest Dreams manifest before your believing eyes! In the course of the next six chapters, you will learn how to identify your Dream, believe in it, and make it come true. Join me on this mystical, practical journey into creating the greatest life you could want for yourself. You can have anything you want when you Dream It!"

Drake raised his head and smiled. He looked like a kid at a magic show.

"Thoughts?" He closed the book.

What I thought is that it sounded exactly like the *Living through Life Changes*, and *Making the Most of Middle Age*, books my mom had on the coffee table. Still, Drake looked so happy compared with the past two days, and I really liked seeing him happy. "It sounds . . . cool," I managed to say, despite my Darkness.

"Okay, I'm going to read more." He looked back into the book and flipped forward a few pages. "This is the first activity."

"No, wait. I really need to ask you something," I interrupted forcefully, breaking Drake out of his spell.

"Okay. What?"

Now that I had his attention, I felt suddenly awkward and vulnerable. Asking about Sandy was going to make me sound possessive and clingy. I chickened out. "Did you do the science homework?"

"Yeah, while I was waiting for your phone to be unbusy. I'll let you copy," he said dismissively. "Now will you listen to this activity?"

I nodded.

"Chapter One: Saying It!

"If you want to Dream It and Do It, then the first step takes place on the feet of your tongue. Too many dreams are held back by negative self-talk. We fill up our conversations with reasons why things aren't working. This first chapter helps you start telling yourself and others all the reasons why things will work!

"Before you can visualize your Dream, you have to verbalize your Dream. Our first activity is simple: state your Dream as clearly and boldly as you can. Do it out loud and do it LOUDLY."

Drake looked up at me. "When I started reading *Dream It! Do It!*, I realized something powerful. I felt like things had gone horribly wrong with Japhy. But actually, he *kissed* me. That really happened. He's probably just too scared to admit that he's attracted to me, which is completely understandable in our homophobic culture." Drake kept shifting around on the bed as he was talking. Then he stood up and walked over to the window. "A lot of people have a hard time coming out."

I wanted to pay attention to Drake, his book, and his story about Japhy. But the Darkness was still having a carnival inside my nervous system. I couldn't hold it in any longer.

"How did your Spanish project go?" I blurted out.

"Oh, yeah, the 'Spanish project.' I need to tell you about that," Drake said, still looking out the window. "That girl Sandy's been my partner for *conversación* since the first day, and we've been talking a lot," he said, "mostly in Spanish. So it's pretty much a '¿*Cómo está usted?*' kind of relationship. But then she started asking me other questions. How long am I staying in Hershey? Did I have a girlfriend in New York? Was I taking any more weekend trips back?"

Just thinking about Sandy talking to Drake this way made my fingers dig into my bedspread and my hands try to form into fists.

"I suck at Spanish, and I barely know her, so I gave her short answers, 'one month, no girlfriend, no more weekend trips.' Then, after school today, we were working on our photo essay about Barcelona and she said, 'Drake, since you are new and you don't have any friends here, I thought it would be nice of me to invite you to the homecoming dance. I could introduce you to a lot of people, and I think you should have at least one good memory of Hershey.' Isn't that hilarious?" Drake said, turning around from the window.

Maybe I have a poor sense of humor, but I didn't find it the least bit funny. Sandy inviting Drake to homecoming. Sandy telling Drake he should have one good memory of Hershey. I was so stunned I could have passed out and fallen off the bed.

"I had already told her that I would still be in Hershey that weekend and that I didn't have a girlfriend in New York, so I didn't really have a good excuse for not going."

The walls of the tunnel were vibrating in and out. Did Drake say *yes*? Was Drake about to tell me he was going to homecoming with my archenemy?

"So, I hope you're not mad at me, but I said I couldn't go with her because I was already going with you."

I was still conscious and sitting on the bed. My head did not splash down on my rug.

"I know it's not cool to use you as an excuse. You might want someone else to ask you, or you probably hate lame school dances. We don't really have to go or anything," Drake finished. "It was just the first thing I thought of to say."

My brain struggled to catch up. This wasn't bad news. In fact, it was the best news possible. Not only was Drake not interested in Sandy and didn't want to be friends with her and wasn't going to take her to homecoming, but also, he had just delivered into my hands the perfect backdrop for my revenge.

FORM OF REVENGE	PRO	CON
Reveal to the school that Drake turned down Sandy for Homecoming to take me	Humiliating, public, clear to Sandy and everyone else that I am cooler than her	

"Forgive me?" Drake asked.

"Totally."

"Back to the book?" He held up *Dream It! Do It!*

"Yes," I said in a voice that sounded far away, as if it came from a blimp flying over the house.

"Great!" said Drake, sitting back down on the bed next to me. "Buddy Strong says that you need to start with the first exercise immediately, as soon as possible after you read the instructions. So tonight, we both need to articulate our Dream. Don't worry if you aren't sure what it is you want yet. Just trust your subconscious to articulate your Dream for you, okay?"

I nodded.

"I'm going to count to three and when I get there, we're

both going to say the thing that we want the most in the world. Okay?"

I nodded again.

"Are you ready?"

Third nod.

"One . . . two . . . three . . ."

As Drake said, "To be Japhy's boyfriend," I went with the first lie that my subconscious drummed up. "To be a successful poet," is what I said when Drake counted to three. But that wasn't what I was saying out loud in my own thoughts. The Dream declaring itself loudly inside of my conscious mind was *To get revenge.*

The next day was Thursday. We were two weeks into high school, and it already felt like two years. I was bouncing along beside Drake on the way to school, still drunk on his news about Sandy and homecoming, happily daydreaming about my revenge, when Drake gave me a present—an affirmation for my locker. He had drawn a comic book–style picture of me to look like a photo on a book jacket with a caption that said:

Celia Door. Bestselling Poet

"Buddy Strong recommends affirmations in chapter three," said Drake, riding his skateboard slowly while I walked next to him. "We'll get to it soon."

I already knew that affirmations are positive phrases like "I can do it!" or "My thoughts are creative!" When my dad moved to Atlanta in July, my mom started seeing a therapist who recommended using them. Mom taped affirmations up in the bathroom so that every time I went to brush my teeth I read, "I am worthy of love," or "I am safe, it's only change." They kept multiplying until I had to peek into a little window of mirror to brush my hair.

"It looks just like me," I said.

"Yeah, I love illustration." Drake shrugged. "I draw my own comic book called *BlackJack*."

"What's it about?"

"A guy named Jack is taking a high school math test when he realizes that he has the power to read minds. So he runs away to Monte Carlo where he can play cards—blackjack, obviously—read other player's minds, and wins millions of dollars. But the money doesn't make him happy. So he decides to start fighting crime by using his wealth and mind-reading powers. Jack is fighting his own demons because his entire family died when a boat capsized, but he washed up on shore alive."

I held the drawing in my hands like an ancient artifact. "I should make you one, too."

"I'm not sure I'm ready to have pictures of me and Japhy in my locker," Drake answered, rolling his eyes. "Why don't straight people have to come out? I wish everyone knew what it felt like to make an embarrassing, public declaration about who they're attracted to. Once Japhy and I get together, then I'll have a reason to come out. I'd rather say, 'Hey, everyone, this is my boyfriend,' instead of 'Hey, everyone, I'm gay. Anybody want to date me?'"

"If Japhy is gay, it doesn't seem like he's ready to come

out. Do you think you guys would really just become boy-friends right away?" I asked.

Drake put one foot down and stopped his board. We were less than a block from school. He looked at me with disbelief. "Why would you say that?"

"Well, it just didn't go so well when you tried to tell him—"

"I'm trying to banish negative talk from my life, Celia."

"But, I mean, *realistically*, don't you think—"

"*Realistically!* Buddy Strong says that 'Dream Bash-ers' are people who erode other people's Dreams by say-ing they are unrealistic. I never thought *you* would be my Dream Basher." Drake looked at me like he had caught me trying to drown a bag if puppies.

"I just think it's a good idea to try and stay grounded—"

"Oh, I'm not *grounded*. Buddy Strong warned that other people would want to pull down the ropes on my hot-air balloon." Drake shook his head and stepped back on his board.

"I'm sorry, I was trying to help you by being a voice of reason."

"Now we can add *unreasonable* to the list of things wrong with me," he said. "Forget I even told you about the book." Drake pushed off hard on his skateboard and rode half a block before I could take a few feeble steps after him.

"Drake, wait!" I yelled, but he disappeared into a group of kids who were also making their way to the front doors.

It was probably the worst possible time for Clock to show up.

"Lovers' spat?" His voice came from behind me. I swung around and saw myself staring back at me in his mirrored sunglasses. Clock's dark hair was hanging to his shoulders and brushing the collar on his trench coat.

I scowled at myself in the glasses. "Join the circus and get out of my life already."

"Relax, Weird, I was just trying to hand you the little picture you dropped. Did your boyfriend draw that for you?" Clock held up the affirmation Drake had given me. It must have slipped out of my hand when I ran after him. "Says here you're a bestselling poet. I bet you're real *deep*."

He said the word *deep* in a whisper that made me flush all over. I reached up a hand to snatch the slip of paper back from him, but he pulled it away right as I went for it.

"It's mine!" I yelled instinctively.

"But it's such good advertising for your career as a best-selling poet," he taunted. "I should keep this, and maybe it will be worth something when you're famous." He waved it around my face as he spoke, the way you use a feather to tease a kitten.

"Give it," I managed to spit out as I grabbed for it again.

He pulled his arms back behind his head so that my body was bumping into his as I tried to reach past him for the note. I was practically pressed against him trying to grasp it.

"Hey, hands to yourself, I thought you had a boy-friend!" he said in a loud voice. I wrenched away from him and looked around. Kids were staring at us as they walked past toward the school building. I pulled my hood up over my head and wrapped my arms around my body.

Clock reached out his hand and offered me the drawing. I snatched it so hard that it ripped in half. Then I furiously grabbed the other half and muttered, "I hate you!" before spinning around and stomping off to school.

x x x

It was impossible to concentrate all the way through first period. I toggled between murderous thoughts about Clock and confused feelings about Drake. Sandy Firestone was absent, so at least I didn't have to deal with the added anxiety of having her within pheromone-smelling distance. Mandy was still there, but she made a disciplined effort to act as if I didn't exist, which was perfect for me.

I was hoping to spend the morning gloating that Drake turned Sandy down for homecoming. But did it still count if he wasn't speaking to me anymore?

"Ms. Door, when am I going to see your revised essay on 'We Real Cool'?" Mr. Pearson asked in front of the entire class. "I expected it yesterday."

"Tomorrow?" I mumbled, conscious of everyone looking at me.

"Hood off and articulate, Celia. Now, when can I expect that essay?"

I pulled down my hood and said, "TWO-MAUR-ROW."

"Good. I expect you to keep that promise. Now, let's discuss the theme of morality in *Mockingbird*. Greg." Mr. Pearson pointed.

✗   ✗   ✗

Before the bell rang to end first period, I had made my own moral decision. I decided to do whatever I needed to do to make up with Drake. If that meant wearing healing crystals and chanting Buddy Strong's name around a campfire while balancing a copy of *Dream It! Do It!* on my head, then I would start collecting firewood. I had spent the class working on a poem.

SWEAR

If this time the eggs don't break,
freckling the sidewalk with yolk splatter,
coating the coffee and the paper towels,
dripping all over my white shoes,
I will never again swing the groceries
back and forth all the way home from the store,
singing and jumping the puddles,
until the bag hits my thigh and I hear
something inside of it crack.

The next time I saw Drake was third period in Earth Science. He was already seated two tables ahead of me when I walked in, and he didn't turn around. I had to make it all the way through a discussion of plate tectonics wondering if he would still be my friend. When the bell rang, I dragged my boots over to his table and said, "Sorry about being a Dream Basher."

Drake stacked his books and looked at me seriously. "You're the only friend I've got in Hershey." The blood drained out of my body and was replaced with liquid silver. We were still friends. He looked down at his hands and then looked back up at me, his brown eyes wet and his eyebrows pulled together. "Do I seem crazy to you for thinking I can be with Japhy?"

My heart flapped its wings hard in my chest.

I held up three fingers in imitation of the Girl Scout pledge. "I don't think you're crazy, and I will never bash your Dream again."

He stood up and we put our arms around each other's shoulders to walk, bumping backpacks as we tried to squeeze through the science door without letting go.

CHAPTER

20

Chapter Two: Strategizing It!

Congratulations! You gave a voice to your Dream. Now that you have LOUDLY proclaimed what it is you want to manifest, it's time to start prepping yourself for the moment your Dream comes true. Remember, luck favors the prepared.

Make a list of things you can start working on today that will ready you for the arrival of you greatest hopes. For example, if your Dream is to travel the world, apply for a passport. If your Dream is to have a million dollars, open a second bank account. Make a strategic list and start checking things off.

Drake handed me *Dream It! Do It!* at lunch so I could start reading chapter two. It was another hot day in September. Thanks to global warming, eating lunch outside is possible more and more days of the year in Pennsylvania. Maybe if we keep indiscriminately burning fossil fuels, we can have pool parties during Christmas break.

"I already started," said Drake. "Sorry to get ahead of you." He took a piece of notebook paper out of his pocket and handed it to me.

Drake's Strategy for Getting Japhy

1. *Get in shape. (Skate more, play basketball.)*
2. *New clothes. Haircut?*
3. *Read books on coming out, prepare for "the talk."*
4. *Ask Mom and Dad to invite his family over for dinner next weekend.*

I had to be careful about how I responded. I couldn't look like a Dream Basher again. "You're going to talk to him next weekend?"

"He won't answer my calls, but if my parents invite his family over, Japhy's parents will make him come. I'm not ready to see him this weekend. I need another week. But if I can just get in the same room with him, he won't be able to ignore me." Drake stood up. "You work on your list while I get in on this game."

While he was standing there putting his strategy back in his pocket, I wrote across the top of a notebook page, large enough for him to see:

Celia's Strategy for Becoming a Poet

Drake walked lazily out onto the court, hiding his enthusiasm from the other players. Something changes in boys between sixth and ninth grade. I know all about puberty and what physically *changes*, but their personalities change, too. In high school you can almost smell the testosterone eating away at their brains. One of the best places to observe this hormonal phenomenon is during the lunchtime basketball game. Only ten boys get to play in each pickup game, so there's lots of jockeying for position. First, two guys step forward to be team captains, juniors or seniors on the varsity squad, leaders no one would challenge. Then they each choose four guys for their team.

A JV player told Drake that Coach Scott wants them to play at lunch for extra practice, so those guys always try to get picked. Joey Gaskill is there every day, stalking about the court with a wallet chain hanging from his waist. He hasn't said anything to me since our exchange at the lockers, but he glares at me in the halls.

During the captain selection, Drake generally mills about in the back of the group or else he takes a long time getting to the court so that he arrives after captains are named. Then he acts casual and disinterested as teams are chosen, even though he is always one of the first three or four boys picked. That day, Clay Applewhite, a varsity star, picked Drake first for his team. When Clay pointed to him, Drake didn't smile or jog over to the captain like some guys do. He just looked up like he had been disturbed from an interesting thought and then walked casually toward Clay.

I was glad Drake left me alone to give me a chance to work on my real strategy. Revenge is a delicate art, like a bank robbery. You don't just write a demanding note and walk into a bank. You have to practice cracking safes, buy your ski mask, gas up your getaway car.

Now that I had the perfect news to humiliate Sandy, I had to figure out how to get it to the students of Hershey High. I couldn't exactly stand on a chair in the cafeteria and yell, "Can I have your attention? Drake turned down Sandy for homecoming!" I needed it to become a headline, a viral video of gossip. That would require a great and devious plan.

Celia's Strategy for Spreading a Rumor

1. *Whisper about going to homecoming with Drake in the halls and make sure a freshman girl overhears us.*
2. *Tell someone and ask her not to repeat it.*
3. *Write it in a note and "accidentally" leave it somewhere.*
4. *Write it anonymously on the bathroom wall.*

A commotion on the basketball court interrupted my scheming. I looked up in time to see Joey Gaskill fall onto his side like a tipped cow. Meanwhile, Drake was turning a one-eighty and dribbling down the court with no one guarding him. He glided undeterred past the players, like he was running through a park full of statues, and finished with a flawless layup. Girls sitting on the grass watching cheered for him. Drake beamed as he high-fived the other guys.

I cheered, too. After all, the more successful Drake was at Hershey High, the sweeter my revenge.

CHAPTER

21

Sandy was back in L.A. Friday morning. She and Mandy were already seated when I came in. I approached their chairs the way a panther approaches a couple of fat, slow rabbits. After all, I was just deciding when and how to pounce.

A new lightness came over me. I pulled off my hood before class started and actually took notes while Mr. Pearson was talking. I raised my hand twice during the discussion on story structure. Every time I spoke, Sandy seemed to cringe like someone was poking her with a needle. She was tapping her manicured nails on the desk, and Mr. Pearson said, "Sandy, stop that."

As the bell rang, Mr. Pearson asked me to stay after class. "I was quite happy to see you participating today, Celia, but you still haven't handed in your paper on 'We Real Cool.'"

I hadn't exactly forgotten. I just didn't feel like doing the paper. I had already handed in the poem, and I felt like that should count.

"I'll just take an F." I shrugged.

"An F would put your entire grade for this class in jeopardy. Why would you fail a class over one paper?"

"I wrote the poem, but that wasn't good enough—"

"A poem is not an essay, Celia, simple as that. I've been lenient because you did turn something in the first time, but this is unacceptable. I expect something on my desk on Monday."

I shrugged again.

"I'm going to need a better answer than that," he said.

"Okay," I managed. I dragged my boots out of the classroom and pulled on my hood.

× × ×

At lunch, Drake chatted on about *Dream It! Do It!* "This weekend I want to go to the public library for some LGBT books," he said quietly after making sure no one was too close to us. "I don't want to check them out at school."

"LGBT?" I said.

"Lesbian, gay, bisexual, transgender," he said. "I already reserved them on the library website. Also, we need to start working on chapter three: 'Seeing.' Come over after school?"

"Can't. Mom's day off again," I answered.

"Pickup time." Drake jogged over to join the other boys on the basketball court. He seemed lighter, too, like he had grown a foot since he found his new book. When we walked home after school, we made it in record time.

✗ ✗ ✗

"Hi, June Bug, I'm in here!" my mom called from the kitchen as I walked into our living room. I cruised through the swinging door to find her sitting at the kitchen table nearly obscured behind a pyramid of papers. There were seven piles of letters, envelopes, file folders, and large mailers, but because the table is round, the piles were mixing together into one giant stack.

"Hey," she said, putting a paper she was holding down on the top of the pile and picking up her coffee cup. "How was school?"

"Fine," I said. "What are you doing?"

"Oh, just getting some finances in order," she answered casually as if I had caught her balancing her checkbook.

I must have given her a disbelieving look.

"Well"—she twisted a finger into her curly mess of hair—"your dad was always better at organizing bills than I was." A pen was tucked behind her ear, and she was wearing her reading glasses. She picked up a sheet of paper and put it right back down. "But that's my challenge now. I'm just going to have to learn how to manage," she said in a lame attempt to sound upbeat.

"Oh, Celia," she added, leafing now through one of her

barely recognizable stacks. "You don't mind if we skip the passes to Hershey Park this year, do you?"

Hershey Park is our town's main attraction. It has roller coasters and waterslides and mascots made to look like happy chocolate bars or friendly peanut butter cups. We've gotten season passes every year since I was old enough to walk, but Dad always said that it was for Mom more than me. When I was really little, she rode rides while Dad and I drank chocolate milk shakes and waited for her. She was more excited than I was when I got tall enough to ride with her. Dad would still sit and hold Mom's purse and our jackets.

"It's just another expense, and I figured you're probably too old for that now, aren't you?" my mom asked, pulling me out of my memory. She was talking to me but she was looking at the bills.

"Oh yeah," I said, feeling Dark. "I'm too old."

"We just need to find places to trim the fat," she added, punching numbers into her calculator with the pen from behind her ear. "That's kid stuff to you, right? You never liked the rides."

"I'm going to go check my email," I mumbled.

"Okay," said my mom, picking up another sheet of paper. "Oh, I forgot." She suddenly looked up, slapping one hand on her forehead. "I meant to defrost a chicken for dinner. I'll do it right now." She jumped up to open the freezer.

I slipped down the hall to my bedroom, starting to feel the familiar black hole opening up in my chest. When the black-hole feeling comes, all the light gets sucked out of the room and into a Dark place inside me. I wasn't sure why the loss of the Hershey Park passes made the Dark feeling come. It's not like I actually *believed* that my dad would come back from Atlanta, and we would all go drink milk shakes and ride rides and be a family again. But not getting the passes felt final, like we were canceling the *chance* that it *might* happen.

I closed the door behind me and opened my email, hoping for something to distract me. Since it was Friday, I had communication from my dad.

Re: Hello, Celia

From: James Door (jdoor@cocacolacompany.com)

Sent: Fri 9/17 9:53 AM

To: Celia (celia@celiathedark.com)

Hi, Turtle,

Last night I checked out bookstores in town. You're going to love the one called Outwrite. They invite authors to speak. I can't wait for your visit at Christmas.

Please remind your mom about the pipes in the basement that we were planning to insulate before winter.

Love,

Dad

The jury is still out on whom I blame for this separation. On the one hand, it seems pretty clear that my mom was the one who "needed time," or "had things to sort out," or whatever her latest vague term for not wanting my father around sounded like. But he's the one who took a job in another state and packed up twelve boxes of his stuff, which looks a lot more like abandoning the family than my mom not wanting more kids. Then again, Mom could have gone along and kept us together as a family, or at least let me go with my dad and therefore escape the miseries of my outcast life in this chocolate-coated town. Most days, I wasn't sure where to direct my anger.

I replied to my dad.

Re: Hello, Celia
From: Celia (celia@celiathedark.com)
Sent: Fri 9/17 4:27 PM
To: James Door (jdoor@cocacolacompany.com)

hi, dad,
you told me you were having a trial separation. so, how's the trial part going?
celia

I had an email from Dorathea:

Re: Friends
From: Dorathea Eberhardt (deberhardt@berkeley.edu)
Sent: Fri 9/17 10:39 AM
To: Celia (celia@celiathedark.com)

hey, celia the dark,

it's hard not to get dragged into the drama of your

parents' breakup, especially when you're an only child.

mine strung me along for years, breaking up and getting

back together. they would always start talking about

reconciliation around the holidays, and then, come new

year's, they hated each other again.

i know loads of people who are queer here at Berkeley,

which is a more inclusive term than gay. the word "gay"

sounds binary, like it's an on/off switch and you are either

gay or you're not. humans are complex sexual beings and

there are lots of ways our attractions and sexual identities

can manifest.

what do you think about being a freshman? promise me

that you won't let high school beat the creativity out of

you. the american education system is increasingly focused

on improving results in biased standardized testing and

not on teaching techniques that inspire creative or critical

thinking. we learned about it in my social justice in the

classroom course. fight standardized testing!

d

When I was eight and Dorathea was thirteen, she and my aunt and uncle came for Christmas. The previous summer she had gone to a camp focused on art as a social movement, which made a big impression on her politically. She had very recently cut her hair short and gotten into wearing men's ties as a fashion statement. Dorathea always had natural beauty that even made poor styling decisions look edgy.

Back then, I was into Barbie dolls. I had a collection of twenty-five, along with a Barbie dream house, a Barbie van, a Barbie VW Beetle, endless containers of Barbie clothes, and a Barbie portable wardrobe. I spent a lot of time in my room playing with them. They all had personal histories and complex relationships. Often their debates involved the scarcity of Ken dolls.

So my parents gave me three new Barbies for Christmas. One was a beach girl with four choices of bathing suits and feet that could snap into flip-flops. Another wore ball gowns and went to the opera. She came with opera glasses and a mink stole. The third Barbie was a businesswoman with a desk, office chair, and practical suit. After we finished opening presents on Christmas morning, Dorathea and I went into my room to play with my new stuff.

That Christmas, she had requested that she be given only books, so her presents all fit in a stack. My new Barbies were piled on my bed. "Look carefully, Celia," said Dorathea, pointing to the mound of corn-silk hair and

plastic bodies. "Look at the way your culture enforces gender stereotypes on children."

I looked. I just saw Barbies.

"If you were a boy, they would be giving you toy dump
trucks and Hot Wheels. But you are a girl, so they assume
you are into playing house and taking care of babies and
dressing up."

"But I really like playing with—" I tried to say, but
Dorathea interrupted me.

"Celia, I think it is time that we made a statement," she
declared. Dorathea decided we should pack up all of my
Barbies, old and new, and put them in a box in the back of
my closet. (Actually, she wanted us to pack them up and
give them away, but I negotiated her down to the closet.) It
was a really hard thing to give up, especially because these
Barbies were new, but it seemed important to Dorathea,
and Dorathea was my only relative even close to me in age.
She seemed so much older and wiser, I just went along.

That night at dinner, the two of us wore outfits that
she considered "gender neutral," consisting of jeans with
white T-shirts. My mom made beef stew served over a bed
of mashed potatoes for everyone except Dorathea. As a
newly affirmed vegetarian, she was eating a grilled cheese
sandwich and carrot sticks. Dorathea kept looking at me
and finally nudged me under the table.

"I've been thinking," I piped up. The whole family
looked at me as I started into the statement we prepared

in advance. "I've decided that I don't want to play with Barbies anymore." I tried to sound full of conviction.

The adults at the table exchanged uncomfortable looks. My uncle let out a deep, obvious sigh and took a large bite of mashed potatoes. My aunt watched him for a minute. Then she looked at my parents. My mom looked back at her like they were communicating telepathically.

The tension in the room was as thick as chocolate syrup. At times when you're a kid it feels like adults are all in on a huge secret that makes them act weird about things that aren't a big deal. I knew that I had said something important, but I didn't know what.

"Well, Celia," my dad said in his head-of-the-household voice. "That's fine. We won't buy you any more dolls. Is there some other kind of toy you would like instead?" My dad was so gentle when he said that. He didn't even sound mad that he had just bought me three Barbies and I said I didn't want them.

I had no idea what to say next. I was making a political statement about not playing with dolls, but I didn't know what I *should* want to play with. I looked at Dorathea, but she refused to look back at me. She just took a bite of her grilled cheese and played innocent.

"Ummm," I said, searching around for the right thing to say. "Hot Wheels?" I finally muttered.

My uncle laughed right out loud at that. He even spit

a little wad of mashed potato on the table. My aunt shot him a silencing look and then she said, "Well, Celia, I would love to buy you some Hot Wheels."

"Yes, June Bug," my mom agreed. "We will get you whatever kind of toy you like." Then she and my aunt both got up and started clearing plates off the table.

The next day Dorathea went back to Oregon, and I got the box out of my closet. My parents never mentioned it again, and for my next birthday, they bought me a Barbie convertible.

CHAPTER

22

All you need is one friend and suddenly a weekend looks like a wide-open field. I ate cereal on Saturday morning while reading my earthworm book. Mom was already at the hospital.

x   x   x

"Oh, hello dear," said the woman who answered the door at Drake's house. "You must be Cecelia." Drake's grandmother was dressed in black pants and a black silk shirt. A thin, yellow scarf circled her neck and then dropped down past her belt. She was unlike any grandmother I had seen. My mom's mother died when I was little, and my dad's mother wore mostly clothing that was themed for the season. She had an impressive collection of snowman sweaters.

"Um . . . *Celia*," I said sheepishly.

"Of course." She took me by the wrist and guided me through her screen door. "Are you hungry?"

"I ate cereal at home."

Drake's grandmother's house was pristine but welcoming. Her sense of home decor seemed to have stopped developing around the time of lime-green velour couches and lamp shades with fringe. The living room rug was so thick, I thought it would be impossible to hear a footstep, even from a fat man wearing boots. Every surface had a crystal candy dish filled with various hard candies.

"I'm so pleased that Drake met a friend in Hershey. He needs someone to spend time with besides an old lady, doesn't he?" She elbowed me in the side like she had just made a funny joke. Then she looked at me for a moment with her eyebrows raised, maybe expecting me to make conversation. I put my hands in the pocket of my hoodie.

Drake emerged from the hall, holding his backpack in one hand and *Dream It! Do It!* in the other. I wondered if he had already been reading it that morning. "Library, Gran," he said, giving her a kiss on the cheek and motioning for me to follow him out the front door.

"Come home smarter," she called as we left.

"We have so much to do." Drake pulled open the garage door to get his bicycle. Mine was parked on its kickstand in the driveway. "First, library. Second, your house to make Vision Boards."

"Vision Boards?"

"Chapter three," said Drake. "I've got all the stuff we need."

Since Drake had reserved his books online, we were in the library for only a few minutes to check them out. Still, two librarians said hello to me. I felt proud taking Drake to the library, like I was introducing him to my friends. "I looked for other books by Buddy," Drake said, "but I guess that's the only one he wrote." I noticed Drake had started to call the author by his first name.

After the library, we rode back to my house. Drake said Vision Boards might be messy, so we decided to work in my basement, which is unfinished. My basement is one large, concrete rectangle with a hot-water heater, a washer and dryer, a utility sink, and a door that leads to the back-yard. My dad slept down there for two weeks before he left for Atlanta. So there's a rug, a futon, a lamp with a glass base, and an old television perched on a coffee table.

"Nice lair," said Drake, turning in a circle around the room. "This place has potential."

Despite the warmth outside, the basement was chilly and smelled like wet towels. We spread out the supplies on the coffee table, including magazines, glue sticks, scissors, and tagboard. Drake reached into his backpack and pulled out *Dream It! Do It!* and started flipping through dog-eared pages. The last few times Drake had read to me from the book, his voice had taken on a serious tone as if he were reading from a religious text. This time was no exception.

"**Chapter Three: Seeing**

"Most people say that seeing is believing, but I say that Believing is Seeing. Average people want to see tangible proof that something is achievable before they believe that it is possible. Well, I can't see electricity, but I believe it turns my lights on! Exceptional people allow themselves to Dream of the seemingly impossible.

"Start by making a Vision Board. Let your subconscious, creative brain take over as you select images that conjure up your Dream Future. Want to buy your Dream House? Put it on the Vision Board! Want muscular biceps? Put them on the Vision Board! Make it visually appealing and make it yours!"

Buddy Strong uses a lot of exclamation points in his writing. I don't think excessive use of exclamation points is the sign of a very good writer. He also utilizes capitalization in odd ways, but I guess that's Buddy's poetic license.

"Okay, let's do this!" said Drake as if all the preceding psychobabble had contained clear and straightforward instruction.

"Do what?"

Drake gave me the village idiot look. "Just cut pictures out and glue them down," he said, handing me a pair of scissors and an O: *The Oprah Magazine*. Following Drake's lead, I started flipping through pages and saw an ad for nail polish with fifty painted nails, an ad for vinyl flooring, two pages of medical warnings about collagen injections, an ad for mouthwash, and a photo spread featuring rain-coats. Nothing in these pages was speaking to any inspiring visions of my future. I closed the magazine and put it down on the futon beside me.

"What's the latest with *BlackJack*?" I asked, hoping to distract myself and Drake from the project.

"Catching a diamond smuggler."

"What made you think of diamond smugglers?"

"Some world terrorism is funded by the illegal diamond trade," he answered, sounding distracted. "Terrorism is big in comics right now."

"Is Superman fighting terrorists?"

"Who cares?" Drake rolled his eyes. "Superman is lame. Anyway, I'm not really working on *BlackJack* anymore. I'm working on *Dream It! Do It!* now."

Drake turned over the image he had clipped and started rolling the glue stick in meticulous circles over the back. Then, he flipped it over, smoothing it down onto his thick piece of tagboard. It was a picture of the Manhattan skyline.

"New York," I said, trying not to sound disappointed by his first image.

"Yep," answered Drake brightly, "that's the first part

of my Dream. Well, I mean, that part's already a reality. This time next month, I'll be back there, starting at an arts school."

"Oh. You made it off the wait list?" Drake hadn't mentioned that he had gotten in anywhere.

"Not yet. My parents said that the school rosters were still full as of yesterday. Dad said he thinks it looks doubtful, but I know that doubt cannot compete with optimism. I still have two weeks, and I have a positive *feeling* about it." I was nearly positive that Drake was quoting Buddy Strong on the power of optimism.

"So what would happen if you didn't get in? Would you stay here?"

"Well, no way could I go back to the school I'm zoned for. They have permanent metal detectors and pat downs for weapons every morning. I don't think it's known for being especially gay-friendly. It's basically arts school or nothing."

"Nothing?" I said, aware that Drake had just called Hershey *nothing*.

Drake looked up at me. "Sorry, lame thing to say. I just meant that New York is where I *belong*, with Japhy."

There went my heart down the elevator to my stomach. It's so easy to get used to being happy, and it's so hard to remember that it's temporary. I picked up the *Oprah Magazine* again, flipping through perfume ads and luscious photographs of cakes.

"I finished the poem about the whale today," I said, tearing out a picture of an aquarium in an elegant home library.

"Oh yeah," said Drake. "Did you think of a good last line?"

Last lines of poems are the hardest, and I had told Drake I was struggling with this one.

"I decided to end the poem with a homophone. It's a word that sounds exactly like another word, but has a different spelling and meaning," I explained. "So, I'm going to end a poem about a whale with the word *wail*."

Drake snorted. "Homophone, as in 'Hello, Homo Phone . . . Drake speaking,'" he said in a lispy voice, which made me laugh so hard I snorted, which made both of us laugh. I put down my magazine and lay down on the futon, staring at the ceiling.

"Will you come visit after you go back? Like at Christmas or something?"

"Jewish, remember? We always go to Florida over the break to visit my other grandmother. But we come to Hershey every summer."

"I'll be in Atlanta then," I said. "And for Christmas, too, I guess. And spring break." It didn't seem possible that I would really be spending every school break in a condo in Atlanta, Georgia.

"Weekends?" Drake suggested.

"Yeah, weekends," I said. We were both quiet for a

minute. I think it was dawning on both of us that we might not have a lot of chances to see each other after he left. "Do you worry about making friends in your new high school?"

Drake didn't stop gluing. "Not really. Japhy will be my boyfriend, and arts school will hopefully have cool people. It shouldn't be too hard."

I would give anything for Drake's confidence. Still, he seemed so sure he and Japhy would be together, but Japhy wasn't even returning his emails. It felt like a stretch, but I couldn't say anything. I had made a vow to support his effort. Plus, they did kiss. Maybe they *would* get together.

"We need to find you some friends for when I leave," Drake said. "What about that guy Clock? He likes you."

"Clock!" I pulled myself up to sit. "He doesn't like me, he *hates* me."

Drake gave me an incredulous look. "Oh, straight guys don't know how to show girls they're interested. Everybody, act surprised." Drake did jazz hands while holding his scissors.

"But he's horrible," I said, a strange mix of feelings rumbling around my stomach. "Don't you think he's horrible?"

"No. I think he's kind of cool. He's unique."

"I didn't think *any* guys liked me," I said, crossing my legs.

Drake put his magazine down and looked at me. "Do you really not get how pretty you are?"

"I'm pale and flat-chested and—"

"Celia," Drake interrupted again, "negative self-talk." Drake stood up and took both of my hands to pull me off of the futon. He led me over the utility sink where an old mirror was hanging on the cement wall.

"Look," he said to me in the wavy reflection of the glass. I took my eyes off Drake and looked. Drake pulled my hood down and gently removed my ponytail holder. He smoothed my dark hair around my face and glasses. Then he pulled my shoulders back from where I was slouching, forcing me to stand up straight.

I don't expect a modeling agency to call offering me a contract any time soon. But the way Drake was looking at me in the mirror was making me look again. I was surprised by how much I looked like my mom. Standing there with his hands on my shoulders, I felt like a different Celia. We stood, his fingers resting on my arms, staring at ourselves staring back from the glass. Drake bent over and whispered in my ear, "Seeing."

CHAPTER

23

We finished our Vision Boards and decided to keep them
in the basement, because I wasn't interested in my mom
knowing about my subconscious Dreams, and Drake felt
uncomfortable with the idea of his grandmother finding
his. Drake's completed Vision Board featured a Manhattan skyline, the image of two men holding hands, a fire
escape, and the words THIS IS IT, along with various things
in pairs: pairs of socks, mittens, two coffee cups touching
handles. It was pretty appealing. My Vision Board however was a messy compilation of books, brick libraries, letters cut out to spell POETRY, and, for no apparent reason,
a puppy. "My subconscious knows," I told Drake when he
asked about the dog.

x   x   x

"Going to Drake's house," I said to my mom Sunday
morning as I pressed through the swinging door into
the kitchen. She looked tired from working a double on

Saturday. She was sitting at the table in her robe drinking coffee.

"To do what?" She asked.

"Stuff," I answered.

"Um, I love doing *stuff*. I never get to do *stuff* anymore," she said sarcastically. "Working the swing today, so I'm going in at two." She sipped her coffee and looked down at the paper spread out before her. "Can you make your own dinner tonight? I'm busy this afternoon."

"Sure," I said uneasily, remembering again how I was too old now for Hershey Park. There was something else I had been thinking about since making Vision Boards with Drake. "Am I really going to Atlanta for Christmas?" I asked, grabbing an apple out of the fruit bowl and taking a bite.

"Well, we haven't gotten you a plane ticket yet, but that was part of the agreement your dad and I made," she said, putting her coffee cup down on the table and looking at me. "Wouldn't you like to see your dad?"

The black hole feeling started. "Yeah." I took a bite. "But why can't he just come home? Half of his stuff is here and isn't this supposed to be a *trial* separation?"

"Please don't talk with your mouth full, Celia. That might be a possibility." She looked into the mug between her palms. "Your father and I should probably have a talk and see if that sounds like a good idea at this point."

A familiar anger shot through me. "So you'll just have

a private meeting and then pass down the verdict to me. Great. Be sure to keep me informed," I said, opening the trash can and throwing my half-eaten apple hard into the bottom.

"Celia, you're wasting food! And, you know that goes in the compost," she said, getting up to open the trash can and pull the apple out.

"Arg." I turned and pushed hard on the swinging door back into the dining room.

"Wait a minute," my mom called as I headed for the front door.

I put my hand on the knob and refused to turn around to look at her.

"Home by seven at the latest," she said. "You need time for homework. I'll call to make sure you're here."

"Any other orders?" I asked.

"Have fun today," she offered in a nice voice.

I just turned the knob and left.

x x x

I biked to Drake's house again and made it there by ten. We had planned to go to the mall so he could buy some new clothes as part of his self-improvement plan to win Japhy. I don't go to the mall very much. My mom offers to take me shopping, but I prefer to buy most of my clothes at thrift stores, since I don't want to have the same pair of jeans as every other girl in school.

For our trip to the mall, I was wearing a pair of green pants from the army/navy store that I rolled up around my ankles and a red-and-white-striped shirt. I didn't put my hair in a ponytail. After looking in the mirror with Drake last night, I decided to wear it down.

Drake met me in his driveway, looked at my outfit, and said, "Look who discovered color."

We pedaled to the mall, which was much farther than the library. A light rain started to fall as we locked up our bikes outside Nordstrom. We made it all the way to the makeup counter before we spotted two classmates, Vanessa Beale, from my French class, and Damian Poole, a freshman who went to my middle school, walking past the perfume display.

Drake pulled me behind a rack of handbags so they wouldn't see us. He held a purple patent-leather clutch in front of our faces and said, "Do you think they're on a date?"

"I've never seen them hang out before."

"Spy?" Drake suggested.

We followed Vanessa and Damian out into the mall at a safe distance, stopping periodically to fake window shop. One of us would watch them while the other pretended to inspect a glass vase or gaze into a jewelry case.

"They're stopping at the Orange Julius stand," Drake reported from our position at the front window of the shoe store while I took a hard look at the soles on a pair of

Mary Janes. "They look like they are negotiating payment. Super awkward." I started to look up at them, but Drake said, "Don't look!" so I *accidentally* dropped the shoe and bent down to pick it up.

"Okay," Drake said, his lips barely moving, "they're ordering the drinks and . . . yep, he paid for them. Definitely a date."

It is such a relic of the past the way boys are expected to pay for your Orange Julius when you're dating. It's very 1950s America. Now that my mom and dad are separated, my dad sends a check every month. When we went out for our last meal together before he moved, they split the bill.

"Would you buy Japhy's Orange Julius if you guys were dating?" I asked Drake, following Drake into the Hot Topic. We gave up on Damian and Vanessa when they went into the movie theatre.

"We don't really have malls in Manhattan," Drake said. "But *when* Japhy and I are dating, we *will* buy each other lots of beverages."

We shopped through a row of fishnet stockings and studded wristbands. "Would Japhy like you in this?" I asked, pulling out a tank top made entirely out of zippers.

"Only if I wore it with these," he said, grabbing a pair of purple metallic boots with yellow soles.

"Can I help you find something?" a salesgirl wearing blue lipstick and Cleopatra eyeliner asked in a monotone voice from behind the sales counter.

We both shook our heads, so she went back to talking to two girls who were chatting with her over the register.

"Did you see the movie where the aliens *are* zombies?" one of the girls asked.

Drake and I moved to look at the jewelry and lipstick bins near the counter.

"Ugh, that movie was stupid," the other girl said.

"I know, everything is zombies now. That movie was so gay," said the salesgirl.

"What did you say?" I asked.

The girls looked surprised, as if I had just walked over to their private table in a restaurant and asked to sit down. "We're just talking about the movie with the zombie aliens," the salesgirl said dismissively.

"But what did you call it?" I asked. I could feel Drake shift uncomfortably next to me and take a small step away.

"I said it was stupid, don't bother seeing it," said the girl.

"But you didn't say 'stupid,'" I said, my voice getting a little louder. "You said it was 'gay.'"

"Oh yeah, whatever, I didn't mean it *literally*."

"No, you said 'gay' like that was another word for 'stupid' or 'lame.'"

"A lot of people say that," one of the other girls broke in, "she didn't mean it in a *mean* way. She's cool with gay people."

"Well, if you're cool with gay people, then why don't

you choose another word to use so you don't offend anyone?"

The salesgirl's eyes narrowed at me through her thick eyeliner, and her blue lips opened like they belonged to an exotic fish on a coral reef. But just then, an older woman, who could have been her manager, walked out of the stockroom. The salesgirl glanced at her.

"Sorry, miss," she said in her flat voice with her eyes looking away. "Can I help you with anything else?"

"No thanks," I said, dropping the cheap, anchor earrings I was holding back into their bin and spinning around to leave with Drake behind me.

"I cannot believe you just did that," Drake said when we were back in the center of the mall.

"Can't anyone just say a movie was *bad* anymore?" I shrugged.

Drake stopped, and his sneakers squeaked on the shiny mall flooring. He turned around to face me and then abruptly took hold of my hand and got down on one knee. Putting his other hand on top of his chest like he was about to propose right there under the vaulting skylights, next to the cell phone kiosk, he said, "Celia Door, will you be my best friend?"

A rose garden bloomed in my chest. The roses got as full as they could get and then started dropping their petals, which blew around my ribs in a gentle breeze. I didn't say anything at first because I wanted to see how long those words could hang in the air. *Best Friend. Best Friend. Best Friend.*

"I will," I said at last, pretending to hold a bridal bouquet and then closing my eyes to fling it behind me into the mall.

"Now that's love," the guy at the mobile kiosk said, clapping his hands. We stood up and bowed for him. "Hey, what mobile carrier are you kids using today?"

Drake laughed as he grabbed my hand and pulled me the other direction back toward the movies. "Come on, let's get some clothes, and then I'll buy you an Orange Julius."

Drake started leading me toward a Zumiez store, both of us still laughing about the cell phone salesman, when something shocking plucked me right back out of the jaws of my happiness. Also walking toward the Orange Julius stand next to someone of the opposite sex was a person I never dreamed of running into at the mall.

Quicker than a snakebite, I grabbed Drake and pulled him into the closest hiding spot. We ducked behind a row of lace bras at Victoria's Secret. Breathing heavily and trying to calm my heart rate, I whispered, "That was my mom."

"Your mom! Is she following you?"

"She didn't know I would be here."

"So she's just shopping."

"With a guy?" I felt like I might cry. "Shopping with a guy?"

"Oh," he said. "Well, your parents are separated, right?"

"Trial separation."

"Yeah right, *trial*." Drake tried to peer around the corner of the underwear table toward the center of the mall. "A lot of my friends' parents used the word *trial*."

"Why do you mean?"

"Everyone knows that's just a phase. Like, they aren't ready to say *divorce* yet, so they do it in stages. Trial separation, separation, divorce," he said matter-of-factly, still peeking out of the store.

The black hole started widening again. Drake turned back to me and noticed the look on my face.

"Oh, shit. Sorry. Well, I'm sure *some* people get back together. Probably *lots* do," he corrected himself.

"Can I help you two with something?" A petite woman with intense blonde highlights peered at us over the bras.

"No," I said in a Dark whisper.

Drake peeked around the corner again to make sure the coast was clear and then we walked as quickly as possible out of the mall.

CHAPTER

24

One thing I need to make as clear as a windowpane is that I do *not* write love poetry. Whenever a girl at my school writes poetry, like for an English class or for the school literary journal, it's always about how much she loves her perfect boyfriend or about how much she hates her imperfect ex-boyfriend. That poetry makes me want to vomit until there is nothing left in my insides. In the spirit of female liberation, I, Celia the Dark, vow that I will never write love poetry.

Additionally, here is a list of the eight words that I believe should never be used in writing poetry: *love, soul, heart, dream, sad (sadness), pain, awesome,* and above all other words that should not ever be used in poetry, *beautiful. Beautiful* has been so overused in poems that it has no meaning anymore.

I call this my list of "Never Words." A week before ninth grade started, I wrote them on my bedroom's lavender wall in marker to make sure I would never use them by accident. My mom came in while I was writing them. I was kneeling on top of my writing desk, wearing a sweat-er, a plaid wool skirt, and knee socks.

I was halfway through writing the word *heart* on the wall when she walked in. I had already written *love* and *soul* in letters two inches high. There I was caught red-handed with an *H* and an *E* on the wall. Usually my mother knocks, but that day she just walked right in, hold-ing a stack of clean laundry.

I braced myself against my writing desk, sure that she was about to scream. That's what a normal parent would do. I just kneeled there holding on to my desk, waiting to hear it.

Instead, she let out a deep sigh. That sigh seemed to come all the way up from her toes. Then she said, "Celia, I don't allow you to write on the walls." Ever since my mom got her therapist, I could practically hear her counting to ten whenever she gets angry: . . . *7, 8, 9, 10.* . . . "You can write on the walls in the basement if you feel you need to."

The reason I don't use "Never Words" is that everyone uses them, and poetry should sound unique for each per-son who writes it. Whenever I'm tempted to use one of my "Never Words," I just try to find another more interesting word to use in its place. For example, if I want to say

the rain made me sad

instead I might say

the rain washed all the color out of my day

It was raining on our bike ride home from the mall.

"Are you okay?" Drake yelled from under the hood of his jacket, cycling next to me.

"No," I yelled back. My hands and feet were numb, but I didn't appear to be bleeding from any visible wounds, so that was a good sign.

"Are you going to confront her?"

"I don't know."

Drake pointed to a sheltered bus stop along the side of the street. We pulled our bikes up, got off, and leaned them against the wall. Then we stood under the overhang while the rain kept pounding on the roof.

"I was stupid to say that," Drake told me, wiping the wet hair from his forehead. "Lots of people have breaks and get back together."

"No, you're right, I—" I couldn't seem to finish the sentence.

"Celia, I really think you need to start working on manifesting your own Dream. The more energy you put into yourself, the less you'll worry about what your parents are doing." Drake put a hand on my arm. "You Dream of being a famous poet. That's what really matters. Promise me you will start on your list tonight."

A surge of guilt pulsed through me. I finally had a best

friend, and I was lying to him about my deepest desire. But I was in too far. What if I told him the truth now, and he didn't want to be my best friend anymore? Plus, he was leaving soon, so why risk ruining the time we had together? "You're right, I should work on my own Dream."

"Tonight?"

"Tonight, I promise."

✗ ✗ ✗

It was still raining lightly when I came home to my mother-less house. Drake and I had waited for the downpour to pass before finishing the ride home. I took off my wet shoes and jacket and walked around in circles, bedroom, kitchen, living room, hall. I tried hard not to think about my father, about how quiet the house sounded, about my mom and what she was doing at the mall. Instead, I decided to follow Drake's suggestion and steady my mind on my Dream.

At school, I had created a dummy list of strategies to make myself into a famous poet. I had to start making progress so Drake would believe I was working on it. The first item on my to-do list for my fake Dream was to submit one of my poems to our school literary magazine, *Nexus*. So, I finally stopped pacing and put a frozen pizza in the oven, then went to my room and got online. I logged on to the *Nexus* website and sent in the poem about the whale.

WHALES ARE NOT FISHES BUT MAMMALS

when a whale gives birth, her vertebrate
back contracting toward her tail, blood
sending valentines to the sharks,
the ocean is her hospital.
she uses her body to
hold the baby up out
of the water so he can breathe.
his blowhole sounds like his first wail.

I also checked my email. Unfortunately, there was one waiting from my dad.

Re: Hello, Celia

From: James Door (jdoor@cocacolacompany.com)

Sent: Sun 9/19 11:39 AM

To: Celia (celia@celiathedark.com)

Hi, Turtle,

I'm glad you asked about the trial part of our separation.
I think we should talk about this in person. I'll call your
mom and see if we can arrange a weekend for me to
come back to Hershey.

   In the meantime, I want you to know that I'm doing okay
down here in Atlanta, and I hope you and Mom are happy,
too. I miss you, Turtle.

I Love You,

Dad

His email seemed to reinforce my worst suspicions, especially the part where he said he was doing okay in Atlanta. I didn't reply. Instead, I wrote to Dorathea.

Re: Parents

From: Celia (celia@celiathedark.com)

Sent: Sun 9/19 6:59 PM

To: Dorathea Eberhardt (deberhardt@berkeley.edu)

d,

i saw mom at the mall with another guy. does that mean she's on a date? if she is on a date, and she and dad are in a trial separation, is she cheating? what if she's only hanging out with this guy, but she likes him? is that cheating or do you have to be at least kissing the other person? what if dad is in atlanta and he's happy and he doesn't care if she's on a date? then is it cheating?

c

I did my math and science homework and fell asleep. I didn't even think about working on "We Real Cool."

"Did you know that the organized gay rights movement started in New York City?" Drake was riding his skateboard next to me on our way to school Monday morning. He was wearing skinny jeans and a bright green hoodie with white zipper and strings. I was wearing a plaid wool skirt and a blue sweater, along with my black hoodie and fingerless gloves. It was the third week in September, and the air was full of fall. "Police were harassing queer people in Greenwich Village until riots broke out at a bar called Stonewall. After that, gay people started organizing and demanding equal rights. Maybe I could take Japhy there."

Drake's skateboard made thumping noises every time he rolled over a crack in the sidewalk. "Also, the books I borrowed from the library say that the average age of people coming out now is sixteen," Drake went on, "and that lots of people don't come out immediately but wait until they feel like the time is right."

"Did you read anything that will help you talk to Japhy?" I asked.

"Not yet." Drake skated quietly for a minute, looking toward our school building a block away. "But I will." We continued on to school.

I removed my hood and floated into first period, feeling like I had grown an exoskeleton over the last few days. I had a best friend and a paved, tree-lined avenue toward revenge. It was easier to table my anxiety over seeing my mom at the mall while I was at school. After all, my real Dream required my attention.

Sweeping gracefully into my seat behind Sandy, I saw her whispering to Mandy across the aisle. Mr. Pearson started class with a brief lecture on responsible use of prepositions and then asked us to write a paragraph about our homework reading assignment. I rushed through the paragraph and got out my poetry notebook to finish a poem I've been working on about Drake. I was so engrossed, I didn't notice Sandy get up and walk to Mr. Pearson's desk. I did notice Mr. Pearson standing over me.

"Hand it over," he said, holding his palm below my chin.

I slapped my poetry book shut and reached for my backpack.

"I didn't say *put it away*, I said, *hand it over.*" He snapped his finger and held out his palm again.

My mouth went dry and my hand shook. Not my poetry notebook. Anything but that.

"I'm sorry, I won't get it out again," I stammered.

"I didn't say *apologize*, I said *hand it to me*." He sounded like a monarch, irritated with one of his subjects.

I sat there like an ice sculpture, not blinking.

"Now, Celia."

Barely able to will my arm to do it, I handed him my notebook.

"I will keep this journal until you complete your assignment on 'We Real Cool.' Since it is now one full week late, instead of a three-page essay, you owe me a *five*-page essay, double-spaced, twelve-point font." He stalked back to his desk, opened a large drawer, and dropped my notebook into it before slamming it shut. Then he sat down again, as if he hadn't just stuffed my heart into a glass jar and sealed the lid.

I couldn't breathe or think. I'm sure my mouth was hanging open when Sandy and Mandy both turned their heads to look at me. All they did was smile.

x   x   x

"That guy's a monster," Drake said at lunch when I told him about Mr. Pearson. "Full Napoleon complex."

I was sitting with a turkey sub in my lap, unable to eat it. I could feel the midday sun on my neck, but I didn't bother pulling up my hood. Everything felt numb.

"You don't think he'll read it, do you?" Drake said.

Maybe I wasn't entirely numb, since that sent another stabbing pain into my chest.

"Are you going to be okay if I go play in this game?" he asked gently.

I nodded heavily and drew the rest of my belongings around me like a little fortress as Drake walked over to the basketball court. I started to wrap up my lunch since it seemed unlikely that I would be eating any of it. Sandy must have been waiting for Drake to leave, because she and Mandy walked through the grass in their high heels just minutes after the game started. I saw them coming, but had no poetry notebook to use as a hiding place.

"So pathetic the way she follows him around." Mandy didn't try to conceal who she was talking about.

"He told me he's going back to New York," said Sandy. "What's she going to do then?"

"My mom says that her dad left," said Mandy. "Not surprised."

I couldn't hold it together. Mentioning my dad was like using a baseball bat in a boxing match. I grabbed my backpack and jumped up, abandoning Drake's stuff in the grass, and took off toward the closest set of doors to the main hallway. I navigated around groups and through couples, making my way as fast as possible to the girls' bathroom and into the first open stall. Dropping my backpack on the floor, I pulled the end of my sweatshirt sleeve down over my hand and stuffed it into my mouth to conceal the sound of sobbing.

I thought I had tough enough skin to keep Sandy from

getting to me now, that turning Dark had protected me from her. I leaned my head against the cold metal of the stall wall and cried so hard that there were barely any tears. I beat one side of the wall with my fist and the other side with my foot. A vicious anger spread over all the skin on my body like a rash, growing hot and itchy from my scalp to my toes.

I took a few deep breaths and pulled a Sharpie out of my backpack. Then I wrote this in the bathroom stall while wiping the tears off my cheeks.

Sandy F. asked Drake B. to homecoming & he said NO!

It was time to pull the trigger on my revenge.

CHAPTER

26

After school, I had to go home and start my paper for Mr. Pearson. Mom was working the swing shift, so I didn't have to worry about seeing her after the incident at the mall. Still, concentrating long enough to write a five-page essay felt impossible, but I had no choice. I couldn't survive without my poetry notebook. I sat down at my computer to spout English class jargon about "We Real Cool," but my mind kept running back over the school day. By the end of lunch, I had visited every girls' bathroom and written the same line in at least one stall in each. I could only hope that somewhere, a rumor was beginning to take. I churned out two pages about how the poet uses rhyme and meter to display themes of disenfranchisement in youth, blah, blah, blah, but there was no way I was getting all the way to five.

I got an email back from Dorathea while I was working.

Re: Parents
From: Dorathea Eberhardt (deberhardt@berkeley.edu)

Sent: Mon 9/20 5:57 PM

To: Celia (celia@celiathedark.com)

celia,

parents do a lot of things when they are trying to "find themselves." after her divorce, remember how my mom changed her name from alice to alyce? she told me she traded in her "housewife name" for her "artist name." now she spends all her time in the attic with her oil paints.

my dad is wearing his midlife crisis like a badge of honor: blonde girlfriend, sports car, condo in los angeles, the whole nine. we're not talking right now. until he is able to acknowledge his white male privilege, I can't deal with him.

maybe your mom is just spending time with different people, trying to figure out who she is. my advice is concentrate on yourself and try not to worry about what they're doing. that's how i got through it.

d

I flopped down on my bed and tried to think of my parents as individual people, and my life as something not connected with their decisions. I imagined my dad in Atlanta with a blonde girlfriend and a sports car, my mom with a boyfriend named *Simon*. I managed to visualize it, both of them in their new lives. The problem was, I couldn't imagine where I fit in. My head was spinning, and my stomach hurt.

Drake and Dorathea were giving me the same advice. Forget about my parents, concentrate on my Dream. I decided not to ask my mom about the guy at the mall. The truth is, I wasn't sure I was ready to hear what she might have to say about it.

✗ ✗ ✗

By the end of Monday night, I still only had two and a half pages of my essay finished. Still, I brought what I had to Language Arts on Tuesday morning. After dropping my backpack next to my chair, I took the paper out of my folder and went to Mr. Pearson's desk, trying not to sound Dark. "I'm almost halfway finished. If I can have my notebook back, I promise to do the rest of it tonight."

"I'm glad that you finally started your paper"—he pushed back his chair and propped his right ankle on his left knee—"although it's a week late and you broke a promise to have it finished on Monday. I need the completed version before I can give back your notebook. I have not been unaware of the distraction it causes you in class."

My left hand clenched into a fist inside my sweatshirt pocket while my right hand held the essay.

"But the original assignment was only three pages—"

"The answer is no. Frankly, if I had known it would be

such an incentive, I would have confiscated your notebook sooner. Back to your desk."

I turned and dragged my feet back down the aisle, while Sandy and Mandy smiled like pageant winners. A hammer in my chest kept pounding the same nail: *Revenge. Revenge. Revenge.*

Before third period, I met Drake by the lockers and walked with him to the science wing.

"Let's go find out the *truth* about the biosphere," said Drake, mimicking our enthusiastic teacher Mr. Diaz.

We walked by one of the orange posters advertising the homecoming dance.

"Hey, Drake," I cleared my throat loudly, as we traveled through a throng of freshmen. "Did you get your suit yet for homecoming?"

He stopped short. A girl bumped into him.

Looking around and then taking a step closer to me, he said, "You actually want to *go*? Red punch, taffeta mall dresses, people you hate in a gym dancing to a bad DJ?"

"It sounds awful," I whispered, "but you told Sandy we were going, so she would know you were lying if we didn't." My plan was backfiring. Now, I didn't want anyone to overhear us talking about homecoming.

"True, but I'll be gone the next week, and I'll never see her again. It was just an excuse." Drake shrugged. "Who cares if Sandy knows I lied?"

I needed to change tactics, so I tried several. "It'll be

lame, but homecoming is still a seminal event in our high school experience," I whispered. "We'll go ironically. We'll be like anthropologists studying American teenagers."

"Does seminal mean what I think it means?" Drake asked. Then he caught the look on my face.

"Okay," he added. "We can go, I guess. It will be my last weekend in Hershey, so it will be cool to hang out with you. Ironically . . . or whatever."

"I'll get my dress this weekend," I said in a robust voice, before subtly glancing around.

Drake gave me a questioning look as he opened the door to science.

✗ ✗ ✗

At lunchtime, while Drake did his usual turn in the pickup game, I sat on the grass constructing a note. In order to make it look like two different people were writing it, I used my left hand to write the responses.

have such good gossip.

w?

sandy f. asked hot new skater guy to homecoming and got rejected!

say more

he's taking dark girl who wears the hoodie

I folded up the note into squares and triangles and crumpled it a little to make it look like it had been read a few times. Then, I got up to walk over the recycling bin to toss in the tinfoil from my sandwich. On the way there, I "dropped," the note in the grass. Then I returned to my spot and put on my sunglasses. Drake was involved in his pickup game, scoring points as usual. I watched the note like it was a dollar bill with a string attached to it, waiting to catch a curious passerby. Through the rest of lunch, sneaker after sneaker walked past that note, a few even stepped on top of it. Not one shoe paused mid-step while the owner bent over to investigate. When the bell rang, I picked up the note myself. I tried dropping it again later in the hall but still wasn't getting any bites. The note idea went nowhere.

✗   ✗   ✗

"In chapter four, Buddy describes our Dreams as tigers. He says that you have to lay the right bait in the forest and then get very still and wait," Drake said, kicking his skateboard along next to me on the walk home from school. "He says it's more effective than trying to hunt a tiger."

"Sure," I said in no mood to internalize any lessons about patience. It was a week and a half until homecoming, and I had a rumor that no one seemed willing to spread and a date who was barely willing to go. I couldn't just sit around and wait for my revenge to take itself.

Truthfully, I didn't want to go to the dance either. An opportunity to hobnob with my classmates over punch bowls and pretzels sounded like torture. I just needed everyone to *know* that we were going. That's the only way my plan would work.

"I called my parents last night and asked them to invite Japhy's family over for Saturday." Drake was focused in the distance, talking toward the trees as I plodded along, trying to keep up. "My dad suggested that we use the weekend to talk about our 'plan B' if I didn't get into an arts school. How can I make him understand that expressing doubts out loud doesn't lead to a positive outcome? If I could just get him to read Buddy's book, he would understand. Maybe I'll bring it with me to New York."

"Is it possible you might stay in Hershey?" I asked, my hands tightened on the straps to my backpack.

"I can't even think about that right now," he said, swerving his skateboard in the graceful shape of an S. "I have four days to figure out what I'm going to say to Japhy. In one of the books I got, it says that queer kids are two times more likely to abuse drugs and alcohol. Do you think that's why Japhy wanted to drink that night? Do you think it's because he can't accept who he is?"

I felt increasingly called on to support Drake's theories about Japhy. "Maybe," I said cautiously. "Sounds believable."

I'm not sure Drake even heard me. "So you really want to go to this homecoming dance?"

"Yes," I lied awkwardly. "I really do."

"Okay. But I'm not wearing a suit. Chuck Taylors and a skinny tie is as far as I'll go. I'm sure Japhy will understand that we're just going as friends."

✗ ✗ ✗

I declined Drake's invitation to go to the wooded lot even though my mother was working the swing shift again. Instead, I forced myself to go home again and eke out three more pages about the metaphorical significance of going to a pool hall instead of high school. By early evening, the shock of having my poetry journal confiscated was starting to wear off, but the time sensitivity for my revenge was growing by the minute. It was time to turn the heat up. The days were wasting.

Wednesday morning, I marched into L.A., dropped off my bag, and then walked bravely to Mr. Pearson's desk to slap down the paper, titled "Jazzing June," five pages, stapled in the upper left hand corner. He looked up from his computer and over his glasses at me.

"Good title." He flipped through the paper first, stopping to read a few sentences in the middle, then opened the drawer where my poetry notebook appeared to be sleeping. He started to hand it back to me, but stopped, then took off his glasses and looked at me intently. "It's clear to me that you are bright and interested in writing," he said. "Your comments in class, when you make them, are incisive and finely articulated. But you don't apply yourself. Why aren't you trying?"

My notebook was within inches of being back, and my hands were in danger of grabbing it without my head's permission.

"I dunno," I said lamely.

"Can you assure me that you will start giving me your full effort?"

"Yes." *Sure. Fine. Whatever. Notebook. Back. Now.*

"Here then," he said, releasing it to my greedy clutches.

I held the binding gripped tightly in my hand as I walked past Sandy and Mandy and then replaced it securely in my bag. I spent the rest of L.A. with one leg resting on top of my backpack.

After class, I went to my locker to exchange books before French, thrilled to see that Becky Shapiro was at her locker, too. Not only was Becky one of the few people I could reasonably appear to confide in at Hershey High, she was also a previous victim of Sandy's malice.

"Hey, Becky," I said sweetly, dialing in my combination.

"Hi, Celia," she replied, adding a nervous laugh.

"The greatest thing happened this week." I didn't look at her as I retrieved my French book from underneath math.

"What?" She closed her locker and leaned on the door.

"Drake Berlin asked me to homecoming," I whispered, standing up and leaning toward her as I said it.

"Ooooh!" She beamed. "I've seen you two together. He's so cute!" She clapped her hands together while balancing her books between her arms.

"I do feel awkward about one thing," I went on, still whispering.

Becky looked around the hall and leaned in closer. "Sandy Firestone asked Drake first, and he turned her down. He told me he would never go with someone so . . ." I paused. ". . . un-cool."

Becky's eyes sparkled like diamonds. "She isn't cool," she said firmly. "Not at all."

"Promise me you won't tell anyone," I added. "I would feel . . . bad if it got out."

"I promise," said Becky back, closing the door to her locker. We both walked off to class.

x   x   x

"So, Mom and Dad invited Japhy's family over for dinner," Drake reported at lunch, "but haven't heard back from them yet."

I was sitting in the grass with my notebook in my lap, carefully smoothing my hands over the cover.

"Buddy says that there will always be reasons to delay going after your Dream. 'The only way to achieve your

Dream is to make your Dream your primary Reason,'" he quoted. I was getting a little sick of Buddy Strong's nonsensical mantras. Drake seemed to have memorized half the book.

I couldn't tell if Becky Shapiro had started the hamster wheel of rumors spinning yet. I did know that the best way to start gossip is to ask someone to keep a secret. Drake and I didn't seem to be getting any more attention than usual. He played in the pickup game, and I sat in the grass, finishing the poem about him that I started on Monday. Sandy and Mandy did not materialize.

✗ ✗ ✗

Wednesday night I had dinner with my mom. We made spaghetti together and ate in front of the television. I did not mention anything about the mall.

Thursday morning, I was getting into my locker before first period when Becky Shapiro showed up. As she started opening her lock, she got my attention. "Did you find a dress for homecoming yet?" she asked sweetly.

"I think I'll look for one this weekend," I said with a lame smile. Even though I didn't know Becky well, I suddenly felt bad about lying to her.

"Well, I wanted to let you know that I didn't tell anyone what you told me yesterday," she whispered. She smiled a genuine smile, proud of keeping my confidence.

"Oh . . . thanks, Becky," I said in a true effort not to sound disappointed. I really needed to cultivate some more devious acquaintances.

Homecoming was one week from Saturday, and my rumor obstinately refused to spread. I needed to take the gloves off. Time was running out. I walked into Language Arts, dropped my backpack at my chair, and was about to sit down when Mr. Pearson called me up to the front of the room. I walked cautiously to his desk. "Celia," he said, handing me back my paper on "We Real Cool." "Excellent essay. This confirms my suspicion that you are not working up to your potential in Language Arts. I expect more class participation and timely assignments from you in the future," he said firmly. "I took off ten points for the lateness, but you still get an A minus." He didn't smile, but looked back at his computer as a way of dismissing me.

Turning back to the class, I noticed Sandy and Mandy whispering behind their hands and glancing at me. I gripped the paper hard between my fingers. There was no time to feel happy about the A minus. I had to concentrate on my revenge. One week away. As Buddy Strong would say, I needed to keep my eyes on the tiger. I walked back to my chair and sat down.

"Okay, class, get out a pencil and one sheet of paper for a pop quiz on the reading from last night, the final chapters of *To Kill a Mockingbird*."

Sandy and Mandy joined the rest of the class in groaning as they cleared their desks for the quiz. I picked up my backpack to get out some paper, then put it down again beside me.

Mandy turned around in her seat to take her purse from where it was hanging on the back of her chair, and pulled out a pencil. As she attempted to rehang the purse on her chair, one of the handles got caught on the edge of her desk and spilled the contents all over the floor. Lipstick and makeup brushes went flying, pens and lip balm,

Mandy's wallet and keys, everything sprayed across the floor. And her cell phone skidded over the linoleum and landed right in front of my toe.

Without a questioning thought or a second's hesitation, I picked up my right boot and crossed it carefully in front of my left one, gently concealing the phone between my two shoes.

Mandy and Sandy both turned around and leaned out of their chairs to snatch items up off the floor as Mr. Pearson said, "Okay, your five-minute quiz begins now." He flipped on the document camera and revealed ten questions about the end of the novel.

"Shit." Mandy frantically grabbed things off the floor and stuffed them back into her bag.

"Spaz." Sandy shook her head while dropping Mandy's lipstick and brushes into her purse, which Mandy then hung again on the back of her chair. They both turned around to start working on the quiz.

My heart was racing. Divine providence had clearly played a part in these events. This must be a sign. The tide was turning and taking my revenge out to sea.

Eyeing Sandy and Mandy to make sure they were focused on the quiz, I gingerly slid both feet, cell phone gripped between them, to the side of my chair next to my backpack. Then, I reached down and exaggerated the action of scratching my leg, while subtly lifting the phone from the floor and depositing it into the pocket of my hoodie.

I flew through all ten pop quiz questions in two minutes.

"Yes, Celia," Mr. Pearson said when I raised my hand.

"May I go to the bathroom? I'm finished with my quiz."

He nodded and I made a heroic effort to leave the classroom casually, dragging my boots all the way to the door. It was all I could do to keep myself from running down the hall. I kept one hand on the phone in my pocket and repeated to myself, "Just breathe, just breathe."

Safely inside a stall and sure I was the only person in the restroom, I flipped the phone open and turned it on. Since students have to power their phones down during class, I could only pray that it wasn't password protected. The light came on, it vibrated once, then a picture of Sandy and Mandy in swimsuits at the beach wallpapered the screen. No password needed. It was real. I had Amanda Hewton's phone.

It wasn't the same carrier as the cell my dad had given me, so I had to tinker with it a little before I could figure out how to create the text message. I couldn't take too long in the bathroom or I'd risk raising suspicions. I typed hurriedly with my thumbs.

had to share the gossip: sandy f rejected by drake b for

hcoming. d says s "isn't cool" & is taking celia d

Then I selected every name I recognized in Mandy's phone from freshman girls to boys on the basketball team.

Clearly, Mandy was gaining some popularity. I saw some names I didn't know and selected them anyway. After a few minutes of pressing buttons, I had texted over a hundred people. And the best part was, they all thought that news was coming from Mandy, Sandy Firestone's soon to be ex-best friend.

I've never smoked a cigar, but I had the insatiable urge to light one up. This was a moment to be savored, an experience to be written about in epic poems that future freshman outcasts would recite at high school reunions. I was Beowulf slaying Grendel. I was Casey at the Bat. I opened the bathroom door and walked back through the hall with an opera soundtrack playing in my mind, my boots moving in slow motion. I had just pulled the sword from the stone.

x x x

Language Arts went on like nothing momentous had just happened in the girls' bathroom. Mr. Pearson was going over the answers to the quiz, which I was pretty sure I had managed to pass, despite my distraction. Sandy and Mandy looked surprisingly smug for two people so stressed out about a quiz. *Enjoy it*, I thought. I had a feeling their happiness would last only until the bell rang and students started turning on their phones in the hallway between classes.

I sat with my hand in my pocket, knowing I had to

make one more calculated compass reading before I was out of the woods. At the bell, everyone stood to leave. Sandy and Mandy surprised me by rushing to exit, but they didn't get out fast enough. There was a bottleneck at the door with students trying to get to the hall, giving me just enough time to position myself behind Mandy and slip the phone back into her purse. The perfect crime.

Once outside the room, I followed Sandy and Mandy toward my second-period class, where a bank of freshman lockers lined the wall. They were walking fast and kept looking behind them, almost as if they were expecting the catastrophe that was about to happen. I stopped outside the door to French and propped myself against a column to watch the students bump and rustle through the halls. Then I closed my eyes and listened through all the voices and commotion to the sound of phones coming on, the beeps and chirps and ringtones of incoming texts, the laughter and repetition of, "Oh my God, did you get it?" It sounded like being in a mechanical forest where all the birds sing artificially. It was the sweetest noise I'd ever heard.

Then I heard Sandy Firestone. "What the hell is this?" I opened my eyes to catch Sandy shoving Mandy hard on her shoulder. They were standing at Mandy's locker down the hall and looking at a third girl's phone who held it out for them.

"Look at the time signature," said Mandy. "It wasn't me. You were sitting next to me in L.A. when this was sent."

That was my cue to disappear. I backed through the door into French, where I happily chatted away with Liz and Vanessa all throughout *conversation*, replaying again the words between Sandy and Mandy in my mind. I tried to mentally translate "What the hell is this?" into French. *"Est-ce que c'est diable?"* People say revenge is sweet, but I would describe it as tangy with a hint of spice, more like pickles or a delicious curry.

I was still full on the intoxicating dish after class when I met Drake to walk to Earth Science. I couldn't resist asking, but tried to act nonchalant. "Did you talk to that girl Sandy today in Spanish?"

"She wasn't there," he said, disinterested. "I still didn't hear back from my parents yet about this weekend with Japhy. What do you think is taking so long?"

"She wasn't there?"

"Who?"

"Sandy."

"No. Why?"

"Oh. That's strange because she was in homeroom," I said. Maybe she was so upset by the text, she went home.

"Bad kid. Must have been skipping," he said, taking a few skips toward science. "If you're worried about her and homecoming, I could just tell her I'm leaving earlier for New York."

"I already bought our tickets," I lied, "so, we should just go."

"Homecoming Saturday, back to New York on Sunday," said Drake, giving me a nod and then opening the door to science.

I tried to concentrate on earthquakes and our terrifying look at the Pacific Ring of Fire during third period, but I had my own internal shake-up to think about. Built-up tension was breaking apart inside me. The release the earth must feel during a 9.0 quake must be fabulous. I couldn't wait to get to lunch and hear all those cell phones beeping again. I looked at Drake two rows ahead and smiled. I had a best friend *and* revenge. What could be better than that? Finally, the bell rang, and I stood to put my science book back into my backpack. That's when I noticed something I didn't see before, something I had been too excited and distracted to take in.

"I can't find my poetry notebook," I said as Drake approached my desk. I was pushing aside the other books and folders in the bag.

"You probably left it in your locker," he said casually, "or one of your other classes."

I started taking books out of my bag, then abruptly turned the whole thing upside down and poured all the contents onto my lab table. Science book, *To Kill a Mockingbird*, two subject notebooks, pens, first aid kit, a glue stick. No poetry journal.

"Time to go," Mr. Diaz said. "I have students taking a makeup test during lunch."

My hand was shaking as I put the books and notebooks back into my backpack. *Don't panic,* I told myself. *Not yet.*

"Meet you on the grass," I said to Drake, and flew out of the room and down the hall toward French, saying a little prayer with each step I took. I noticed students grouped in the hall, looking at a flyer posted on the wall, probably a reminder to vote for homecoming court.

I burst into my French classroom and said, "Ms. Arnold, I think I left my poetry notebook in here during—"

"Celia," she interrupted me. *"Je ne comprend pas. En Français."*

I grabbed my head, willing my brain to think quickly in French. *"Je . . .* lost *. . . mon journal de poesie, et je pense que je . . .* left it *. . . ici,"* I finished pathetically.

Mademoiselle Arnold looked around the room and shrugged. *"Je n'ai pas trouvé un journal, mais—"*

Rudely, I didn't wait for her to finish, but turned to race back to Mr. Pearson's L.A. class, praying he would look at me over his glasses and admonish me for being forgetful as he handed it back to me.

But as I left my French room and started down the hall, I saw what the other kids had been looking at posted on the wall. It wasn't a homecoming flyer. It wasn't a flyer at all. Photocopied onto goldenrod-yellow paper and plastered every five feet along the length of the hallway was a sickeningly familiar image. It was six lines long, and it was in my handwriting. I forced my feet to walk over. Yanking the first one I could reach off the wall, I looked closer. Above a page from my poetry journal, someone had written this.

A POEM FROM THE DEEP AND IMPORTANT
WRITING OF CELIA THE WEIRD...

Since Drake told me that day in the wooded lot,
while the leaves agreed with gravity and left the trees,
that he liked boys instead of girls, it's been easier
to love him. Loving him feels like counting or using
the phone or something else that's effortless. I'm like
a leaf with nothing to do but fall.

I recognized the curly handwriting above my poem instantly. After all, it had tormented me since the eighth grade. I flashed back to standing at Mr. Pearson's desk, receiving my A minus, while my backpack lay unprotected at my chair. I remembered the strangely smug look on Sandy's face after the quiz, and the way she wasn't in Spanish class. While I thought I was so clever stealing Mandy's cell phone, they had taken my poetry journal.

I heard a boy's voice down the hall saying in a mocking high falsetto, "I'm like a leaf with nothing to do but fall." Other boys laughed. The black hole in my chest was growing at an alarming rate. I felt like I might be sucked into it entirely, never to be seen again. The goldenrod paper trembled in my hand, and a few people bumped into me trying to get past.

Something inside of me gave up. Being Dark hadn't protected me. Revenge hadn't rescued me, it hadn't even worked. Now everyone would be talking about the poem instead of the text message, talking about Drake instead of Sandy. I was the same old Celia who could be picked on and humiliated. The only difference between this and the eighth grade was that I had managed to bring Drake down with me. I finally got a best friend, and I had betrayed him to the whole school. After promising I would never tell anyone that he was gay, I told *everyone*. I started melting like a stick of butter. Soon I would be nothing but a puddle on the floor.

That's when two firm hands found my shoulders and a deep voice said into my ear, "You head down the hall and I'll go up." Those hands pushed me firmly toward the wall where the pages were hanging. I looked behind me and watched Clock tear down a yellow page and add it to the stack he already had in his hand. I stared as he walked on to the next one, pushing away a couple of freshmen who were trying to read it. "Oooh, so shocking," he said to them mockingly, "we live in the suburbs and we don't know any gay people." He tore the paper off the wall right in front of them.

As if someone had held smelling salts up to my nose, I came to life. I turned to go up the hall in the direction of the library, pulling down posters furiously as I went. "Excuse me," I said rudely, pushing people out of my way. "Just collecting my intellectual property." I tore my poems down like they were old birthday streamers. "Correcting copyright infringement," I barked, stomping into the next hall, which was also coated in copies.

I yanked down twenty more photocopies before I thought of Drake. What if he had seen them? Or worse, what if he *hadn't* seen them and was innocently sitting on the grass eating lunch, just waiting to be humiliated? I tore down three more of the posters as I raced off through the building toward the outdoor picnic tables.

Comments bounced through the hall as I ran. An upperclassman said, "Is that her?" and pointed. A freshman boy yelled, "I agree with gravity, too." There was plenty of general laughter. I just wanted to get to Drake and explain what happened, to tell him about the poem before he saw it on the wall. I hit the door to the lunch area and ran past the picnic tables to our usual spot on the grass. To my dismay, Drake was already on the basketball court with the other boys.

I stopped at the edge of the asphalt, praying for the gift of telepathic communication. It wasn't like I could run onto the court and talk to him in front of everyone. Reacting to the drama any more would only make it worse.

They were still choosing teams. Drake appeared to be deep in thought, but I couldn't tell if it was his normal reserved demeanor with the boys or if he was thinking about how much he hated me for telling the whole school he was gay. Would he be playing the pickup game if he already knew? Was he trying to be cool, act unaffected, or was he completely unaware of what was posted in the halls?

Clay called Drake's name as he picked him for his team. Also looking absorbed was Joey Gaskill, who got picked last for the other team.

I stood helplessly on the side of the court as the game began. Drake played better than usual, with more aggression in his stance. When he guarded another player, his eyes bored into their elbows and his hands pushed roughly at the ball. The players' long bodies spread out over the court like starfish. The offense turned into arrows while the defense transformed into shields. When someone stole the ball, all the players would shape-shift again, shooting themselves one way or the other down the court.

Drake was guarding Greg Baker, a sophomore on the JV team who was in my gym class. Drake blocked all of Greg's attempted baskets, but every time Drake went for a layup, the ball might have been a magnet. He couldn't miss. Drake scored ten points before anyone else on either side had a basket.

There were more spectators than I had ever seen for a pickup game. Hershey High's version of a celebrity scandal was enjoying a public moment on the blacktop. "He doesn't play like a fag," I heard a boy say from another spot on the lawn. I tried to look unaffected.

Humans must be natural followers like the famous cliff-jumping lemmings. Actually, it is a misconception that lemmings commit suicide by throwing themselves off cliffs in mass numbers. I learned about it in a book from the public library called *Mythical Anthropomorphism: Urban Legends of the Animal Kingdom*. What really happens is that as lemmings migrate in large groups and approach a cliff, the first lemmings to the edge try to stop. But the follower lemmings keep crowding in behind the leaders pushing them one by one off the cliff and usually to their deaths.

As the crowd watching the game grew, the game got more intense. A couple of other players made baskets. Drake seemed to grow two feet taller on the court. I was gripping the straps on my backpack so tightly that I had marks on my hands where the nylon was digging into my skin. My hands were sweaty, and my heart was beating hard. Part of me was on that court with Drake. There was no sign yet of Mandy or Sandy, although I kept scanning the lawn for them. I had no idea what I would do if they showed up.

Joey Gaskill's game was off, no steals or baskets. His shirt was soaked with sweat in huge circles around his armpits. One of Joey's teammates passed him the ball, and

Joey made an impressive run down the court, followed by the boy who was guarding him, with Drake and Greg right at his heels. Their four sets of running shoes seemed to fight each other for a place to land. All of them reached the basket at the same time, ringing around it and gazing up. Joey sprung from his heels with one knee in the air for the jump shot. Joey's guard, Greg, and Drake all sprung, too. It could have been a ballet if there was less grunting. They all leapt together.

Just as Joey's hand released the ball into a perfect arc ending at the basket, Drake's hand made contact, halting the ball's momentum and sending it off the court. The bodies of all the boys continued their path back toward the earth, propelling Drake and Joey right into each other as they crash-landed back on the court in a tangle of legs and feet.

Despite his slowness on the court, Joey was the first one off the ground. "Get off of me, you fucking *faggot*!" he yelled, pulling his legs apart from Drake's and hurling the words at him. The crowd went silent, and the words hung in the air like fireworks. They were huge.

Drake shook his head for a moment, like he was trying to brush cobwebs off of his face. I watched his eyes take in the size of the crowd around him. The next second he was on his feet, one arm swinging out to his side like a wrecking ball. It was a wide, wild swing, and it landed on Joey's face like a spaceship splashing down into the ocean.

Joey thudded onto the asphalt. But that didn't satisfy the demon that possessed Drake. He leapt on top of Joey and landed two more solid punches to Joey's torso before other boys jumped in to pull him off.

A roar went up from the bloodthirsty crowd. *"Fight, fight, fight!"* they chanted. I could feel the thrill on every side of me. Their basketball game had morphed into a boxing match. The people on the grass jumped to their feet after the first punch. No one wanted to risk being asked for the details of the fight in their next class and not being able to provide any. After the second punch, kids flooded toward the basketball court, hoping to get a front-row seat for the wreckage.

I had to get to Drake. I grabbed my backpack and started to force my way through the mob. Everyone was pushing. I couldn't see the court anymore for all the tall boys around me. The crowd was like quicksand. I started shoving harder.

I got to the inside of the circle just in time to watch Principal Foster, Coach Scott, and Mr. Pearson finish tearing Drake and Joey apart and then lead them by the arms back into the school building.

I stood in a throng of bored, desperate, horny, mean, giddy teenagers and watched as the best one of us was dragged away to be persecuted.

CHAPTER

28

Schadenfreude is a German word that means "delight in someone else's misery." It's one of the words I learned in the book *Foreignisms*. It is the feeling of thrill we get when we read gossip magazines about a starlet getting a DUI. It's the reason we want to see the mug shot, examine her shame-filled eyes surrounded by dark, half-moons of skin. Sometimes high school pulses with it.

As soon as the teachers led Drake and Joey away, the bell rang for class and the mob outside thinned until I was able to breathe. I considered running, just leaving school property instead of going back inside. But Drake was in there, and I didn't want to abandon him. I pulled the hoodie up over my head, opened the door to Hershey High, and went into battle.

I didn't see any more photocopies of my poem as I walked down the hall. Clock must have gotten them all. I headed straight for Mr. Fish's European History class. I didn't stop at my locker for my book, even though it might mean a lecture from Mr. Fish. A lecture didn't seem like my biggest problem.

I could feel the *schadenfreude* buzzing around me. I heard the names *Drake* and *Joey* repeated by almost every group of students. Two boys were reenacting the fight for a group of girls. There was a carnival atmosphere in the halls, a palpable glee running through the freshman class. A chorus of heads turned to stare at me as I walked by.

I timed my entrance to history so that I could sit down right as the bell rang. That way, no one could attempt to talk to me. My heart was beating so loudly in my ears that I almost couldn't hear Mr. Fish start class. A voice in my head was attempting to sort out what just happened, but Mr. Fish kept drowning it out.

"Okay gang, settle down," he boomed. "Open your books to page forty-three and continue reading the chapter on the French Revolution. I heard we had big excitement at lunch but we are still here to learn."

After giving me a disappointed look when he noticed I had come to class unprepared, Mr. Fish let me borrow a classroom copy of our textbook. I settled in and opened to page forty-three, trying to make it through one paragraph. *"Even after the attempted flight of the royal family, Emperor Leopold von Habsburg of Austria, brother of Marie Antoinette . . ."* I must have started reading that sentence twenty times. The words just looked like words. Nothing made sense.

"Okay, gang," Mr. Fish said to all of us, although I was pretty sure that I didn't belong to the gang. "We are going to continue our section on the French Revolution by dividing up into discussion groups."

Oh no! screamed the voice in my head. Any discussion group I was in wasn't going to focus on the French Revolution. Everyone was going to ask me about the poem or the fight. It would probably be the most popular moment of my high school career.

My hand shot up into the air before I consciously thought to raise it.

"Yes, Celia," said Mr. Fish.

"I need to go to the nurse," I said.

"What for?" Mr. Fish sighed.

"It's private," I said in my most adult voice. A couple of kids laughed. Kids always know when other kids are faking sickness. It's funny that adults don't. He let me go.

The halls were clear outside my class, no students or teachers in sight. I didn't know where I was going, but it wasn't to the nurse. I pulled my hoodie up over my head, held on to both straps of my backpack, and decided to walk toward the principal's office.

Just as I rounded the corner to the main hallway, I caught a glimpse of Drake's grandmother walking in the direction of the main office. I ducked back behind the wall before she noticed me. She was walking quickly, her shoes making clicking noises on the floor. I waited there until I couldn't hear the shoe sounds anymore and then peered into the main hall again. I wasn't surprised the school had called Drake's grandmother; fighting was a serious offense. They probably called his parents, too.

A kid holding a pass walked around the corner and past me. If I kept standing in the hall, I would risk seeing more students, or, worse, a teacher. It was time to make a decision. I had no intention of going back to history class and facing other kids for two more periods, and I couldn't get to Drake while he was in the principal's office. I did the only thing I could think to do. I turned into the main hallway, walked to the set of doors that led to the side of the building, and exited into the daylight.

My boots thumped against the concrete on the familiar walk from school to our neighborhood. I reasoned that if they called Drake's grandmother, they were probably sending him home with her. We all knew the penalty for fighting. *Suspension . . . expulsion*, both words contained the terrifying sound of *shun*. I had to get to Drake, to tell him what happened, to help, to do *some*thing. I planned to walk to his house and wait for him to get home.

All I could do on the twenty-block-long march was wonder what was happening at school. Was everyone talking about the poem, about the fight, about Drake or me? Would it just be the freshman class, or would the whole school be interested? I thought about what happened in eighth grade when Sandy started the Book. I couldn't go through that again, and I certainly couldn't watch Drake go through it. Not because of me.

Drake's grandmother's car was already in the driveway, so she must have taken a different route since I didn't see her drive past. I was on the sidewalk just outside of his house when she opened the door.

"Hello there, Celia," she said, but not in a nice-to-see-you voice. "I'm sorry, dear, but Drake can't talk to you right now. He is grounded. I have unplugged his computer, so there will be none of this emailing." She managed to make emailing sound sinister. "And I have taken this." She waved Drake's cell phone over her head. "Shouldn't you be in school?"

"Is he okay?" I asked, choosing to ignore the question about school.

"Pfft," she said, throwing up her hands. "Can a child be called *okay* who is hitting other children and breaking noses?" So Joey Gaskill's nose was broken.

"Will you tell him I stopped by?" I asked in my most not-Dark voice.

"I'll tell him. If you aren't going back to school, you'd better go home." She shook a finger at me.

I turned toward my house. It's just like adults that when something traumatic happens, and the thing you need the most is to talk to your best friend, they decide to punish you by not letting you talk to your best friend.

I looked hopefully at Drake's window, my brain spinning like a Ferris wheel, then walked a little farther along the sidewalk and paused by a neighbor's lawn two houses down. The house next to Drake's had a wooden fence surrounding it, but the house next to that one didn't. There were no dogs or people moving around, so I ducked down and ran along behind the first neighbor's fence in the direction of the wooded lot. Then I circled around to the back of Drake's house and crouched down behind a bush to look for evidence that his grandmother might still be outside. Finding none, I crept right along the side of the house to Drake's window and pelted it with a tiny stone.

No answer.

I picked up a larger rock and tossed it. The curtain drew back, and Drake's head appeared at the window. I chanced a wave. He looked at me and shut the curtain again. Picking up a larger rock, I was just about to target the glass a third time, when the window opened. Drake leaned out and whispered, "Hold on," and then pulled his head back inside.

I waited behind the bush, trying to figure out what to say to Drake. I would have to tell him about the poem, if he didn't already know. My intestines tied themselves in a bow. After a few minutes, the window slid open again, and Drake looked out. "I was on the phone with my parents," he said irritably in a loud whisper.

"Are you in trouble?" I asked.

"Are you for real? Yeah, you could say I'm in trouble." As the sun caught Drake's face, I could see a bruise starting to form over his right eye. Joey must have gotten in at least one punch.

"What did they say?" I asked, postponing the thing that *I* had to say.

"They're more worried than mad, it's not like I've ever gotten in a fight before. But I'm still grounded . . . and suspended." His head disappeared inside the window again and then came back. "I thought I heard Gran."

"So, I wrote a poem—" I finally started, but he cut me off.

"You mean the poem that outed me to the whole school? Yeah, I'm pretty familiar with that poem, nice imagery with the leaves," he said in a sarcastic whisper. "It was so great to read that on the way to lunch with other people standing around. That was awesome." So he did know. His voice was dripping with rage.

"My poetry journal got stolen—" I started.

"I don't fucking care if it got stolen. Why would you would write a poem about me being gay and then bring it to school and leave it lying around! That's either stupid or . . . just . . . stupid." He was gesturing with one hand while the other clutched the windowsill.

"It wasn't lying around, it was in my backpack. Drake, I would never—" I started.

"He called me a *faggot* in front of the whole school."

"You already knew about the poem, and you still played in the game?"

"What was I supposed to do? Hide in the bathroom? Act ashamed? I'm not ashamed." Drake ran a hand through his hair and then rested his head in that hand.

I sat there in miserable silence.

"I'm so sorry—"

"My parents said I can't come to New York this weekend." He let out a long sigh. "They said they want to come here instead and talk to Principal Foster tomorrow. Mom's trying to get the day off."

"But you're supposed to see Japhy this weekend."

"Yeah, no kidding. What am I going to do? I *have* to go to New York," said Drake, slamming one hand on the sill and then glancing nervously back inside the house. "I need to talk to Japhy. He's the only person who can understand." Drake whipped the back of his hand across his face and winced when he touched the bruise. "Ouch, fuck. If I could just see him, he would look at my face, and he would know how hard it is coming out. He would know that I understand the way he acted."

A dog started barking a few houses away. I tried to conceal myself more fully behind the bush. "Maybe they will let you come up next weekend," I offered.

"Timing is everything, Celia. Dreams have a ripeness just like fruit, and you can't let them rot on the tree," he said. He didn't credit Buddy, but I was pretty sure he was quoting. "Getting outed at school, the fight. It's a sign. I need to go talk to Japhy *now*. I can't wait."

"Maybe your parents will change their minds?"

"No, I can't risk asking permission."

"I am so, so sorry, Drake," I said quietly, overcome with guilt again. I pressed my body into the bush and resisted the urge to cry. There was a silence.

"Come with me."

I shivered.

"I'm leaving for New York tonight before they get here tomorrow. I'll get in trouble, but I'm already in trouble. After Gran goes to sleep, I'm sneaking out. Come with me," he said again.

"I'll get suspended if I skip tomorrow," was the first of ten reasons I thought of for why I shouldn't go.

"I'm already suspended. There are worse things."

"My mom would freak—"

"We're not running away. We can call your mom as soon as we get there, and we can stay at my family's apartment. I've got my keys. We'll never be in actual danger."

"What happens when our families wake up and call the police to declare us missing?"

"We can leave some kind of note, something they'll find once we're on our way and they can't stop us."

Drake was leaning farther out of the window, both hands now supporting him on the sill. His eyes were red and bloodshot and his nose was running. I could almost feel how sore his face must have been.

"We'll need money," I tried.

"I use Mom's credit card to buy all my train tickets. I'll buy yours, too."

"I . . . I don't know."

"Our Dreams are going to require bravery—" He turned his head sharply and then disappeared inside again. When he came back, he said, "The phone's ringing, it's probably them. Come back at twelve o'clock. Gran goes to bed at nine, and she takes her hearing aid out, so you can knock on the window," he whispered quickly. "I checked the schedule and we can get the bus to Harrisburg and make the five a.m. train. Coming, Gran," he called into the house. Then he looked back at me and said, "Twelve o'clock . . . please come," before pulling down the window and closing the curtains.

I collapsed into the bush and sighed.

After a few deep breaths, I made my way back along the side of Drake's house and then through the neighbor's yard and back to the street. There was still an hour until the final bell rang, and I had to kill time at the park so that I wouldn't get home before school was out. I sat on a swing and thought about going to New York and wished I had my poetry journal to comfort me. It made my skin crawl to think about Sandy and Mandy reading it.

I had exhibited some shocking behavior since high

school started two weeks ago. I had ignored assignments, got detention, stolen a cell phone, forged a text message, and just now, skipped all my afternoon classes. But nothing compared with going to New York without my mom's permission. This was another level of bad.

As the swing moved back and forth, I weighed my options. I would be in a mountain of trouble if I went. But I owed Drake in a huge way after outing him at school. Still, Drake was planning on moving back to New York, and I would still be here with a probable suspension and angry parents to deal with and no best friend. On the other hand, if I was grounded after Drake was gone, it's not like I would be missing out on any social time. I would have nothing to do anyway. I swung back and forth, while my brain did laps around a track of my skull.

Finally, when I had wasted enough time to get dizzy, but not to make a decision, I walked home.

x x x

My mom's car was in the driveway. I knew she was working the night shift and wouldn't need to leave for hours. I prepared myself for parental small talk, hoping I hadn't gotten busted for skipping my last three classes. Not every teacher takes attendance. When I opened the front door, I found my mom standing at the coat closet.

"Oh, hi, June Bug," she said. "How cold is it out there? I was just trying to decide which coat to wear."

"Um, medium," I answered cautiously, throwing down my backpack inside the door. So far, so good. That's when I noticed we weren't alone. There was a man with blond hair and horn-rimmed glasses sitting on our sofa. He stood up when he saw me come in.

"Celia," my mom said brightly, "this is Simon, my friend from the hospital. Simon, this is my daughter, Celia."

Simon offered me his hand to shake and smiled widely. I did not smile back, and I did not shake. It was the guy from the mall.

"Mom, is he a date?" I asked in a Dark voice.

"Celia!" My mom snapped. "Don't be rude. Can I talk to you in the kitchen for a moment, please?"

I followed her through the swinging door with my hands folded across my chest. "That was snide, Celia. Simon is the first friend I've made at the hospital, and you just embarrassed me."

I thought about how people kept assuming that I was dating Drake, but he was just my friend. "Is he gay?" I asked.

"No, he isn't," she said, sighing. "Enough with the rude questions. He's a friend and that is all you need to know. Simon came over to have dinner and go to a movie before my night shift, and I was wondering if you would like to join us."

I felt something finish hardening inside of me, like water that can officially be called ice. There was a decision hanging over my head when I walked through the door and, in that moment, I made it. "Mom, I have a ton of homework, I'd really rather stay home," I said.

She stood looking at me. "Are you sure? I'm afraid that I leave you to eat alone too much. We're going for Difari Pizza, and I know you love that place."

"Yeah, that does sound great, but I have a big paper due," I said casually. "I'll just have a turkey sandwich here."

"Okay," she relented. "Bed by ten o'clock. No later."

"I didn't mean to be rude," I said, smiling. "Sorry."

"Well. Thank you, Celia. That is very nice of you to say." She patted my arm and looked at me curiously.

I followed her back into the living room. "Nice to meet you, Simon," I said, waving. "Have fun tonight."

"Nice to meet you too, Celia," he said, standing up from the couch again and waving back.

"Have a good night, June Bug," Mom said, and put on her coat. "I'll see you in the morning."

"I'm going to school early to hit the library before English, so I might leave before you get home."

"Okay." They left through the front door.

Then I went to my room to start packing for New York.

CHAPTER

29

I pulled out a duffel bag and started with socks and underwear. Then black leggings, black T-shirts, a couple of black skirts, and an extra hoodie. I added the novel I had started reading, *Looking for Alaska* by John Green, and begrudgingly found a brand-new composition book to start another poetry journal. It made my bone marrow boil again to think about Sandy and Mandy reading my poetry. But I couldn't afford any more thoughts of revenge. My glorious revenge had gotten me exactly fifty minutes of satisfaction before Sandy did something worse to me. And she hadn't just aimed for me this time, she'd targeted Drake, too. Instead of tossing another grenade, I needed to focus on triage.

I went to my computer. Although I was reasonably alienated from both of my parents, I had no desire for them to sit around thinking I had been abducted by a biker gang or polygamous sect. I thought of someone safe I could tell.

Re: Your eyes only
From: Celia (celia@celiathedark.com)
Sent: Thur 9/23 4:05PM
To: Dorathea Eberhardt (deberhardt@berkeley.edu)

dorathea,
For a good and just cause that would take way too long to
explain, i need to go somewhere for a day or two. i will be
perfectly safe. i'll be with a friend.

I'm not going to ask mom and dad for permission, but
I don't want them to worry. will you wait until after 10
a.m. tomorrow and then tell them i'm safe and i will get in
touch with them? i can't say where I'm going, but i can say
that i have to go.
THANKS!
celia

I got up from my computer and flopped on my bed.
There were seven hours between Drake and me. I made
a to-do list that included: make sandwiches, find money,
shower, nap, and try not to panic. I managed all but the
last two. I was panicking too much to take a nap. I remembered that my mom keeps emergency cash in the freezer,
because if your house burns down, the refrigerator might
survive. Imagine a ranch house burned to ashes, and the
milk is still cold on its shelf. I brushed the ice crystals off
three hundred dollars and concealed it in several locations

on my person. After that, I spent some agonizing hours staring at the ceiling and checking the clock, and then it was finally quarter to twelve.

Grabbing my duffel bag, I left through the front door. The neatly manicured sidewalks of our subdivision with their flat slabs of creamy concrete transformed into an eerie stage set at midnight. Directors of horror flicks know there is nothing creepier than exaggerated perfection. The streetlights alternated lighting up sections of the road every few minutes, and televisions flickered in a few dark houses like strobe lights. I had never been in the neighborhood by myself this late at night before. With every step I took away from my house, I felt like my life belonged a little less to my parents and a little more to me.

I took the same path behind the neighbor's fence to Drake's backyard. Instead of tossing a pebble, I stood in the flower bed and knocked on Drake's windowpane. His grandmother's house, like mine, is just one story, so all the bedrooms are on ground level. As soon as Drake had opened the window, he leaned right through and hugged me. He had to hang halfway over the ledge to do it.

"I knew you would come," he whispered. Even in the darkness, I could see that the bruise on Drake's cheek had gotten darker.

I passed him my duffel bag, and he helped me climb over the sill. Luckily, Drake's grandmother's house has a brick façade, and it's pretty easy to find a foothold on brick.

"My first break-in," I said as soon as I was safely in his room, dusting off my skirt and hoodie from climbing through the window.

"Most robbers aren't given a hand getting over the sill," Drake replied. He suddenly gripped both of my arms and looked into my eyes. "What is the title of the fifth chapter of *Dream It! Do It!?*"

"Um, I dunno," I said, feeling awkward about the way he was looking at me.

"Fearlessness," Drake repeated back. "The first three lines go like this." Drake closed his eyes like he was channeling a spirit. He recited.

"Chapter Five: Fearlessness

"You are Dream Warriors. Your Dream demands that you move boldly through the world. This is the part where you stop Dreaming and start Doing!"

"The bus leaves for Harrisburg at two a.m., and it gets in around four." He went to his desk drawer and produced a train schedule. "Then the train for New York leaves at five, so we'll be stuck at the station for a bit. I'll bring cards. We can buy our train tickets to New York once we get to the station. The earliest train of the day never sells out, even on a Friday. My parents are planning on getting the train that comes in from New York at ten."

Drake walked over to his bed and put the train schedule into the backpack lying there. *Dream It! Do It!* was on the bed, too, lying open. It was my first time in Drake's room, which, in truth, didn't look like a teenage boy's bedroom so much as a grandmother's guest room that a teenage boy was trying to inhabit. The rug was robin's egg blue, and the walls were papered in a deep red fabric. Thick, heavy curtains hung over the windows, and there were two wood dressers and a full-length mirror. There was even a stand with an antique quilt draped over it. The only signs of youth were a pile of sneakers parked next to a skateboard by the door and a bunch of notebooks sitting out on the desk. Drake's room reminded me again that in Hershey, my new best friend was a guest.

"I wish I could do something about my eye," Drake said, looking into his mirror at the dark bruise blossoming there. You could count the individual knuckle prints where Joey's balled fist impacted Drake's face.

"Did it hurt?" I asked him.

"Not as much as you would think." He kept looking in the mirror. "All the adrenaline makes your body numb. It hurts more now than when it happened."

"So, how long's your suspension?" I asked, flopping down on the bed near Drake's backpack.

"Three days," he said. "So school won't notice I'm missing

tomorrow, but Gran will figure it out when she calls me for breakfast. As soon as she realizes I'm gone, she's going to call your mom."

"My mom will think I'm at school when she gets home from her shift."

"They should both know we're missing by around nine," said Drake, "depending how late Gran plans to let me sleep. They won't know where we've gone, so we shouldn't have to worry about getting caught on the train. We'll be halfway to New York."

"Won't Japhy be in school when we get there? How will you get to him?"

"I've been thinking about that." Drake turned away from the mirror to look at me. "I can't decide if it is better to go to his school and wait for him outside until the bell rings, or to kill time until after school and go to his house. His parents would definitely let me in and he would have to talk to me, but he might feel more awkward about seeing me with his parents there. I don't know." A shadow passed over Drake's face. "Buddy will have advice for me. I need to read some more on the train." He picked *Dream It! Do It!* up off the bed and added it to his backpack.

✗ ✗ ✗

When Drake finished packing, he stood in the middle of the room and turned around and around as if he was memorizing the look of each of the four walls. Finally, he picked up his knapsack, turned to me and said, "Okay, Celia, we're going back out through the window."

It was harder getting out of the house than it had been getting in. Still, I perched on the ledge and jumped safely into the grass without snagging my tights.

Drake tossed both of our bags through and then looped two legs over the sill. He got footholds on the brick, gripped the window frame with one hand, and used the other to pull the sash down as far as possible. Then he hopped off into the grass. We made for the street, looking around the way cat burglars do on television shows. Our plan was to walk to the bus depot, since we couldn't call a cab to come to Drake's house. We went the long way, weaving through the neighborhoods and staying off of main streets.

The night air was cold, reminding me that winter would be here soon. We walked quietly for a while past the four different models of houses in our subdivision. The thing about planned communities is that you don't get a lot of surprises. A homeowner is really thinking outside the box if he decides to add a porch or a two-car garage. In Hershey, even the houses just want to fit in. We left the neighborhood and started walking along Cocoa Avenue, cutting through parking lots when possible to avoid being spotted by passing cars.

I switched shoulders when my duffel bag got too heavy and refused Drake's offer to carry it, starting to wish that

I had worn sneakers instead of boots. "What will you say to Japhy when you see him?"

"I keep imagining that moment," said Drake, walking beside me since he had left his skateboard at his grandmother's house. "I think when he sees me with a black eye, I won't have to say a lot. I feel like he will just know. Buddy says that 'your Dream is looking for you as much as you are looking for your Dream.'"

We turned off Cocoa Avenue and then I saw them, blinking through the dark, the fluorescent lights of the bus depot.

Bus stations are not very friendly environments, especially in the middle of the night. We got there just before two a.m., and the station agent looked at us sideways for a moment but didn't seem that curious. Of all the people who are hard to surprise, I bet people who run bus stations are high on the list. Even as we purchased our tickets at the adult rate, swearing that we were over sixteen, the man looked jaded, like he knew we were lying and also couldn't care less.

We sat in orange bucket seats that were connected on a long, metal rail while we waited to board. They looked like something I imagined would furnish the holding room of a jail. The fluorescent lights kept flickering. I half expected the police to walk through the station door and the station agent to point to us and say, "There they are, officer. I knew that girl wasn't sixteen." But it never happened. Instead, the agent announced that the bus to Harrisburg was ready for boarding, and we climbed onto the bus along with ten other people.

Drake and I chose a row in the middle of the coach. The seats were covered with heavy carpet-like material, and luggage racks were suspended over our heads. The windows were as wide as my outstretched arms, but they showed only streetlights and store signs and darkness. I had never traveled anywhere without my parents. Part of me felt like it was the start of a great adventure, like I was jumping on board a pirate ship in a comic book. But part of me felt like a bully had drawn a line in the dirt and dared me to cross it, and I had just walked over and planted both feet. I wanted the moment to be vibrant in my memory, to recall every detail, but as soon as the engine of the bus fired up, I fell asleep. When I opened my eyes again, I saw the redbrick train station of Harrisburg, Pennsylvania.

Drake held my hand as we crossed the bus parking lot and went through the giant glass doors of the station, which is one large hall, like a waiting room built for a giant. The walls are polished wood and there are white columns that appear to be holding up the ceiling on their great, singular arms. Long, wooden benches line the walls.

The station was surprisingly busy for so early in the morning; it wasn't even four a.m. yet. "Commuters to New York and DC," Drake muttered as if he had heard my thought.

We bought our tickets with Drake's credit card and walked to one of the smooth, worn benches to wait until our train left. We had almost an hour to kill until boarding, so we sat cross-legged and played Go Fish because it's a game you could play without having gotten any sleep.

"Do you have any twos?" I asked, halfway into our second game.

"Yes." He handed me two cards. He didn't seem to care that he was losing.

"How about threes?"

"So now everyone at school knows about me," Drake said instead of "go fish."

The statement stung. "I'm so sorry about the poem."

"It was probably Joey that posted it, huh? He's had it out for me." He shook his head. "How could he have gotten your notebook?"

Drake looked back down at his hand and said, "Go fish."

"It was Sandy." I looked up from my cards.

"Sandy?" Drake looked up, too. "But we've been partners in Spanish. Is this just because of homecoming? That's so extreme."

"It wasn't just homecoming," I said. The black hole in my chest opened to the size of a silver dollar. The cards trembled in my hand. "Sandy targeted you because you're friends with me, and she has always targeted me. Since school started, I've been trying to get revenge on her." My voice came out high and thin. I had come so far with Drake: from friends, to best friends, to secret allies, and now runaways. I had waited too long to trust him, too long to tell him the story I hadn't told anyone else. "Revenge for something that happened to me in the eighth grade."

We both readjusted ourselves on the bench, and I finally told Drake the story of the Book.

CHAPTER

30

The day I got the note from my English teacher Ms. Green, the one that said I was talented and my writing was a gift, I started standing up straighter. It felt like being in a public place where you don't know anyone and suddenly, someone calls your name and waves. It was May, a month after Ruth had been dragged from school, and two weeks after my parents had announced their trial separation. My dad was sleeping in the basement, and my mom was working constantly. Ms. Green's note was pretty much the only thing I had going for me.

After Ruth was gone, I used to eat lunch by myself as fast as I could and then go to the library for the rest of the period. At first, I didn't even go to the lunchroom, I just stood by my locker to eat. But I got in trouble with a teacher and started going to the cafeteria. Less than a week after I got the note, I was at a table eating alone when Sandy and Mandy walked over with their sack lunches and sat down beside me. They didn't ask. They just surrounded me like alley cats around a Dumpster, sniffing me up and down.

For one crazy minute, I wondered if they wanted to be friends with me, if they had noticed I was solo and were going to invite me into their clique. Sandy spoke first. "Celia, we've decided to sit with you today because we want to help you." She folded her fingers together in front of her like she was giving a speech and then looked at me with practiced sympathy. Mandy seemed like she was suppressing a cackle, but Sandy looked earnest and intent. They started unpacking their lunches. I took another bite of my sandwich and didn't say anything.

"The two of us got together last night," Mandy said, pulling open the lid on her yogurt and licking the excess from the foil. "And we made a list of things you need to change before high school." She put down her lunch and reached into her oversized purse for a colorful envelope, like one you would get in a set of stationery. She handed it to me. "We're afraid that if we don't give this to you now, you might be"—she moved her hand in a circle framing my face in the air—"like this forever." Mandy popped open the lid on a Diet Coke and looked at me like she was watching a soap opera. Sandy stared at me soberly.

"We're here to help, Celia," Sandy added quietly. "We've done a lot for other people."

I opened the sealed envelope and took out a piece of pink stationery. At the top of the page, someone had written in excessively swirly letters, *Things Celia Needs to Change.*

As I looked at it, Sandy said, "I think you should read it out loud. That would probably be the most helpful thing." She sounded like a school counselor, like she had my well-being at the front of her thoughts.

I did exactly what I used to do before I turned Dark, whatever anyone told me to do. I read the paper out loud.

This is what it said:

Things Celia Needs to Change
1.) *Hair. Get it cut every three weeks (we suggest long layers) and use a brush every day. You're going to need a de-frizzing product, too.*
2.) *Clothes. Places you should shop: Bruno & Basso, Mode Celeb, Hotheads. Places you should not shop: Goodwill.*
3.) *Friends: Try to make friends with some girls before the end of this year. Even if you don't keep them for high school, you need a starter clique for the first few weeks. We suggest Becky Shapiro, Denise Bailey, and Sarah Ellis. (Please avoid religious freaks.)*
4.) *Attitude. You need to stop being a teacher's pet. Nobody likes a brownnoser in high school. Stop acting like God's gift to English class.*
Sincerely,
Sandy & Mandy

They each signed the note with their own signature like it was the Declaration of Independence. I folded up the note, not looking at them. I couldn't see them and control the tears that were inching their way closer to my tear ducts at the same time.

"Do you have anything to say to us? We did spend a lot of our time working on that for you." Sandy said, like it had been a great sacrifice, as if they had just thrown me a surprise party and I forgot to act surprised.

I wanted them to go away. I flashed back to Becky Shapiro in the bathroom when Sandy told her to go on a diet. I knew that Sandy wanted me to say "Thank you," and that saying "Thank you" would make it end. I knew those words would conclude their fun for the day and give them something to laugh about later on the phone. Maybe they really did think they deserved to be thanked. Maybe they truly believed their note was helping me.

But that's not what I did. Instead of that, I looked carefully at each of them and then, channeling Holden Caulfield in *The Catcher in the Rye*, I said, "Fuck off."

Sandy turned bright red. She looked like she was about to take a manicured nail and scratch her initials into my cheek. Instead, a beauty pageant smile lit up her face, and she said, "You're going to wish you hadn't said that."

Sandy didn't take her eyes off of me as she methodically gathered up the items of her lunch, forced them back into her paper bag and stood. Mandy looked like she was in a foxhunt, and someone had just released the dogs. She snatched up her yogurt and her Diet Coke. I wasn't sure what I had unleashed on myself, but fear started forming in my toes and turned into terror as it rose toward my brain. I didn't know what those girls were going to do to me, but I knew it was going to be brutal.

Nothing happened that day. Sandy kept her eyes on me in English class so I didn't raise my hand, even when Ms. Green looked right at me and asked for our thoughts on *Of Mice and Men*. Ms. Green looked at me quizzically when I didn't answer, but she didn't say anything.

The next day was when everything started. I first caught sight of the notebook in science. Mandy was in that class, so it must have started with her. It was being passed furtively from one table to another the way prisoners in a war camp might hand off a stolen spoon. It skipped my table, but I saw it moving. It was a pink notebook with spiral binding at the top like a steno pad.

In every class I had that morning, the book traveled around the room like a cold virus. Every time the teacher's back was turned, it infected a new table, and by the end of class, everyone was sick with it. I ate lunch as fast as possible that day, barely sitting down for five minutes before rushing off to the library.

It went on like that after lunch, too. First, the notebook would get handed to a new person and he or she would curiously open it and read the first page. Next, the reader would look up at me. Then that person would continue flipping through the pages and reading until finally writing something and passing it on. I saw a few people who only read the book and never wrote in it, like Becky Shapiro. There were others.

I tried to pretend it wasn't happening, that kids weren't obviously staring at me over their lockers between class or laughing when I walked by them in the hall. I wished so much I had someone to talk to about the notebook, but I didn't have any friends. I didn't want to go to the principal. The punishment for being a tattletale would probably be worse than what was already happening.

I was walking home from school by myself when I saw them. Mandy and Sandy were standing on the sidewalk a block away from the parking lot. They looked relaxed like they were waiting for some smoothies they ordered to go drink on the beach instead of waiting to ruin a girl's life. I could see it when I was still twenty feet away. Mandy dangled the book from one hand, like a dog bone that she expected would make me run to her faster. I thought about turning around or crossing the street, but why delay the inevitable? I kept walking.

"Hi, Celia," chirped Sandy when I was within taunting distance. "We've got a present for you."

"Everyone at school helped make it," added Mandy.

They both looked so pretty standing there, their long, thin legs stretching out from under their skirts and reaching down to their flip-flops. They wore their hair in ponytails that hung down their backs like velvet ropes. It was a warm day, almost the end of the school year. I wondered why it wasn't enough for them to be pretty and popular. Why did they have to do this to me?

I walked up and stood in front of them, a criminal before a judge. I knew the verdict already.

"Since you wouldn't take our word for it," said Sandy, "we decided to ask everyone at school what they thought you needed to change about yourself."

"This way you can know what everyone is really thinking about you," said Mandy conspiratorially as if she were offering me the answers to a math test.

I had come too far to bother breaking now. "Screw you," I said with a blank look on my face. I didn't offer them any emotion.

"You wish, lesbo," said Mandy as she tipped the book out of her hands letting it thud on the pavement in front of me. She and Sandy pushed me out of the way and walked past me down the sidewalk.

"Some people refuse to be helped," Sandy sighed as they stalked off, their flip-flops beating against the bottoms of their feet like the drums of war.

I had no choice but to pick up the book. I couldn't leave it there for someone else to find. At least if I took the book, I could go burn it or toss it in a Dumpster or use my parents' paper shredder on it. I picked it up delicately between my thumb and forefinger, stuffed it into my backpack, and glanced behind me. Sandy and Mandy had turned to watch me, and they were laughing.

When I got home, I sat in my room alone. My mom had already left for the swing shift, and my dad wasn't home from work yet. They seemed to be avoiding each other as much as possible, with one showing up only after the other one left. I took the notebook out of my backpack and placed it on my desk. It just sat there looking back at me.

I told myself it was a terrible idea to open it, that whatever was written on the pages would only hurt me. But I knew what Mandy and Sandy knew when they gave it to me: I couldn't resist. I had to find out what was inside.

The first page of the book was the same note Mandy and Sandy handed to me, with *Things Celia Needs to Change* and the list of five things. It was glued onto the lined paper.

The new entries started on the next page. They were all written in different handwriting and pen colors like signatures in a yearbook. They were all anonymous.

Try to make friends who aren't fundamentalists.

Celia needs to shave her legs before wearing shorts. Gross!

She should wear clothes that fit her. Her jeans are two inches too short, and she's wearing the same T-shirts she wore in sixth grade.

One word . . . posture.

Learn to cross your legs when you sit down.

Try growing some boobs.

[The next person drew an arrow to the comment above and wrote "jerk."]

Celia just needs to try and fit in.

She should learn to play sports like other ugly girls.

It's hopeless. If I was Celia, I would probably just kill myself.

I closed the book and thought about the story we had read in English earlier that year, *The Fall of the House of Usher* by Edgar Allen Poe, where a family's house gets a crack in it, and the crack keeps getting wider until the house falls down. That's what I had inside of me, a crack. I could feel myself coming apart.

My dad got home around six o'clock that night and immediately started packing boxes in his office. He asked me to help him, but I refused to come out of my room. That weekend, I barely spent any time with my parents. I was reading *The Giver* by Lois Lowry and trying hard to pretend I had another life. They each made attempts to come and talk to me, but I had sewn my mouth up tight, and the seam wouldn't rip that easily.

On Monday morning, I played stomachache. On Tuesday, it was a migraine. By Wednesday, Mom said, "Fine. If you aren't going to school, you're going to the doctor," and I relented and went back to Hershey Middle.

That's when I started learning how to be Dark. I glowered at teachers and classmates and wouldn't raise my hand in class. When people laughed at me or whispered about the Book, I pretended I didn't hear them. I pulled my hood up whenever possible and wore my hair down around my face.

The only teacher who seemed to notice was Ms. Green. "Could you stay after class please, Celia?" she asked a week after I got the notebook. She waited until everyone had cleared out and then sat down at a student desk next to mine. "You haven't been participating in class like you used to. You've seemed a little sad or something, so I gave a call home yesterday. Your mom told me about the separation. Atlanta's a long way away, huh?"

"Uh, yeah, I guess," I said, not actually knowing how far away it was.

"I wanted to give you this." She stood up and got a package from her desk wrapped in brown paper and handed it to me. "I was trying to think of something that might help." I opened it and found a blue journal with blank, creamy pages and the word *Poetry* written in bold letters on the spine. "Creative writing can be a great way to work through your sadness," she said, resting her hand gently on my arm. "You can get out what's inside of you."

I tried several times over the next two weeks to write

a poem. I took the journal with me to lunch and the library. Sometimes I sat in front of it, thinking how clean and lovely the pages were. None of my ideas seemed important enough to vandalize them. Other times, I would think of a phrase or line, but then it would seem stupid, or cliché, something I'd heard a hundred times before. What if I tried to put my feelings on the page and they were pathetic? That would feel worse than being sad. Ms. Green must have been wrong about me.

Finally, in mid June, eighth grade ended, and I hoped I would be able to breathe again. Then, in mid July, my dad left for Atlanta. During the month in between, I tried ignoring my parents, yelling at them, asking politely, and finally begging. I begged that we would all move to Atlanta together. When that didn't work, I begged that I be allowed to go with my dad. They were unrelenting. My mom insisted on staying in Hershey, and she insisted that I stay with her. Through it all, I never cried, even when the car came to take him to the airport and he hugged me and said, "Turtle, I'm leaving Hershey, but I'm not leaving you. I've got a great job down there, and I'm going to make things better for us. I love you."

Even one tear might crumble the new cement that was hardening between me and the world. I just said, "Bye."

Summer never came that year. I'm sure it got hot like it always does in Pennsylvania, but in my memory, June and July were cold. I spent a lot of time staring at the Book that my classmates made. I didn't open it again, but the words written in it bounced around my head like an echo through a canyon. Especially the phrase, "I would just kill myself." Everywhere I went, that phrase followed me. It started to sound like a viable alternative to everything. Like, "I could take a shower, or I could just kill myself," or "I could go make breakfast, or I could just kill myself." The crack that had formed inside of me widened. The color drained out of everything. I stopped going outside, I stopped going to the library. I stopped emailing Dorathea. Then I stopped reading.

My mom noticed, but she would just say things like, "I know, June Bug, it's hard for me having your dad gone, too, but it is necessary. Things will get better." She started seeing a therapist and reading self-help books.

Then, on July 20, the day before my fourteenth birthday, I finally gave up. My childhood was over. My dad had moved, middle school was done with, and everyone hated me. High school would just be more of the same. I decided the book was right. I decided I should probably kill myself.

It was a Tuesday, and my mom was working a double shift, morning and swing. I spent the day thinking about how I would do it. People used sleeping pills I had heard, so that seemed like an option. But we didn't have any in the house. We had no garage, so I couldn't go for carbon monoxide poisoning, and my mom's car wasn't there anyway. We didn't own a gun, and the thought of hanging terrified me. I decided I would do it with a razor blade in the tub.

I started by collecting everything I would need into the bathroom. The only candles I could find were the little ones you put on a birthday cake, so I stuffed them down into the soil of an aloe plant. I found a new razor blade in my mom's shaving kit and some bubble bath under the sink. I got the clock radio from my room and put it in the bathroom so I could play music. I thought something classical would be nice.

I put on a bathrobe and left my clothes in my bedroom. I didn't exactly feel sad or excited, I felt relieved. I was relieved that I wasn't going to have to face anything anymore, relieved that I would never have to go back to school, relieved that I wouldn't have to watch my family break apart. I started the water in the tub and put in the bubble bath. I wanted everything to be clean.

Sitting on the edge of the tub and staring into it, something struck me. It had to do with the way the light was hitting the razor blade. It wasn't a conscious thought; it was more of a feeling coming to me in words. I couldn't shake a phrase out of my head, "The razor reflected the sky like a mirror."

I figured I might as well go write it down. After all, I wouldn't have another chance. In my room, I looked for paper and then remembered the poetry journal from Ms. Green. I had to search through my bookshelf and desk, but I finally found it stashed in the bottom drawer, still blank. I opened the cover and wrote the first stanza of my first poem.

When I felt good about the lines, I went back to check on my bathwater. I had spent so much time finding the journal and writing in it, the water was lukewarm. Something struck me again. I went back to my room and kept writing. When I finished the poem, I added a title.

THE DAY I ALMOST KILLED MYSELF

It was afternoon and the razor
reflected the sky like a mirror. The bath towels
were white like the bathtub and my wrists
were white like the towels.

The bathwater got lukewarm.
The afternoon turned into late
afternoon and I was still pulling ropes of air
into my lungs like a sailor. The razor reflected
the sunset. The bathwater got cold.

The bath towels were white like the bathtub
and my wrists were white like the towels.

I pulled the plug on the tub and ended up taking a shower. That night, I thought about the title of the book

Mandy and Sandy had given me, *Things Celia Needs to Change*. I decided that there *were* some things I needed to change before high school. I also decided that I would be the one to decide what those things were going to be.

The next day I woke up, turned fourteen, and became Dark.

Celia the Dark.

Drake sat there with his hands folded together in a prayer position, and his pointer fingers pressed against his lips. He didn't say anything for a minute.

"Why didn't you tell me?" he asked gently without moving his fingers from his lips.

"I was worried that you wouldn't like me if you knew how much of an outcast I was."

"But I already knew about the Book," said Drake.

"What?"

"Sandy told me about it in Spanish class during *conversación* the second week of school, but didn't admit that she was behind it. Actually, she acted like she felt sorry for you because you didn't have any friends. She had seen us hanging out and wanted to warn me that befriending you would be *social death* for me at Hershey," said Drake, rolling his eyes dramatically.

"But you never asked me about it."

"I figured that you would tell me when you were ready,

and I kept waiting. I was surprised that it took you this long to trust me."

I had kept a terrible secret from my best friend, and it turned out he had known it all along. "I wouldn't have guessed about the other part," said Drake. "The . . . bathtub."

"Yeah," I said, looking down at the polished wood of the bench. It was so hard letting him know I had considered doing something terrible to myself. The black hole was open in my chest, but it wasn't getting any wider. I felt like Drake could see it now, too.

We met each other's eyes. His were brown and tender, like a picnic on a warm day. I was looking at him when something over his left shoulder caught my eye. A woman was walking toward us.

And she wasn't just walking, she was also waving. She became more visible with each step, the way a Polaroid picture develops while you are looking at it. I had never seen the woman before, but she was definitely moving in our direction. She was elegantly dressed in brown pants, a black coat, and high heels. She had a mass of long, dark hair framing her face and falling over her shoulders. She was pulling a suitcase behind her like it was a reluctant dog.

I twisted around to look over my shoulder, thinking that she must have been waving at someone else sitting nearby. Drake turned to see what had my interest, and in an astonished voice, he said, "Mom?"

Drake stood up off the bench and swung around toward the lady. *Busted!* We were caught and we hadn't even made it out of Pennsylvania. How did she find out? I had never met Drake's mom, but knowing parents, I braced for yelling.

She took a few more quick steps and released her bag. "Hi, honey," she said, grabbing Drake and putting her arms around him while he hung limp as a cotton doll. "Are you okay? Does it hurt? Let me see your eye." She put her hand around his chin to get a look at Drake's bruise. "Probably a week to heal; I was afraid it would be worse." She turned away from us. "David." She motioned toward a man in a pair of jeans and button-down shirt who was holding a large, leather bag in one hand. "Over here."

"I told your grandmother we would get a rental car." She turned back to us and then reached out her arms to hug me. "This must be Celia. I'm happy to meet you. Shouldn't you be in school today? Where is your grandmother, Drake?" Drake's mom looked right and left at the other commuters as the man in the button-down shirt walked over to us.

"Hey, kid," he said to Drake warmly, wrapping him in a hug. "Sorry to get you out of bed so early. We told Mom not to come pick us up, so you guys could sleep in."

Again, Drake was stiff, not hugging the man back. "Celia, I'm guessing. Hello," he said cordially, extending a hand to shake mine, "I'm Drake's dad."

Neither Drake nor I said a word. We were like two rabbits in the grass with a snake moving nearby. Frozen.

"Honey, is Gran waiting in the car?" Drake's mother asked him, starting to sound concerned. Then, she looked at him more closely and said, "What's wrong?"

I saw the realization pass over Drake's face at the same time it occurred to me. They didn't know they were catching us. "You were supposed to come in at ten." Drake sounded like a person waking up from a faint.

His dad said, "All the other trains were sold out until this evening, and we needed to get here early enough to meet with your principal. Gran must have told you that."

"Where is your grandmother?" Drake's mom asked again, more forcefully.

"I have to be in New York this weekend," said Drake quietly, as if he was talking to himself.

"What are you talking about?" his dad asked calmly. "We told you we were coming here instead."

"I'm still going, with or without you." Drake started to seem mildly hysterical. He took a few steps away from them.

"Why do you need to go to New York?" his father continued in a calm tone, taking a step closer to Drake.

"Japhy was supposed to come over. I need to talk to

him," Drake said, sounding like he might be close to tears.

"Honey," his mom said gently, "they said *no* for this weekend even if we were going to be there. Japhy's mother had a performance, and Japhy is going out of town with his girlfriend's family."

In old Road Runner cartoons, Wile E. Coyote is always getting an Acme anvil dropped on his head when he tries to concoct a complicated plan to catch Road Runner. Drake and I were coyotes, eyes spinning and birds flying around our skulls.

"Girlfriend." Drake's voice was just above a whisper.

"Drake, what is going on here?" his father asked forcefully. "We didn't expect you and Gran to meet us here. We reserved a rental car."

"Where is your gran?" Drake's mom asked for the third time.

"She's not here." Drake sounded defeated. "Celia and I were going to New York."

"Alone?" barked Drake's dad. "She would never allow that. What the hell is going on?"

"I was coming to New York to see Japhy." Drake's arms hung lifeless at his side like garden hoses. "I'm in love with him."

Everyone was speechless. Drake's parents stared at him with so much concern on their faces, they could have hardened into theatre masks. Then they looked at each other. It was a slow movement as his mother embraced

Drake, and his father hugged them both. Then they melted together, one hugging lump with Drake at the center. Drake's mom and dad both said some muffled words to him while they huddled, but I couldn't hear them.

When they finally pulled apart, they all looked redder around the eyes. "Well, let's go get the rental," Drake's father said when everyone had collected themselves, "and get back to Hershey."

CHAPTER

32

I lost consciousness almost immediately in the backseat of the rental car and didn't come to until Drake's mom was patting my leg and calling to me. "Wake up, Celia," she said gently. "After I called Drake's grandmother, she called your mother, so she's expecting you. They must have been trying to call us when we were on the train and didn't have reception. Everyone was very worried."

My head was resting on Drake's shoulder, and his head was resting on the window. The car was sitting in front of my house. Time to face the music.

I got my backpack out of the trunk and said good-bye to the Berlins, then dragged my boots fearfully to the front door of my house. I was too tired to feel Dark. I stood on the porch and was starting to fish around for my house keys when the door swung open, and there was Mom, a furious Medusa, her curly hair made of snakes, ready to turn me to stone. Red lines crossed the whites of her eyes like tiny bolts of lightning.

"Inside," she said, pointing so hard she might have dislocated her shoulder. She waved at Drake's parents and then closed the door behind me.

"This is it, Celia!" She pointed one finger at me. "I'm done." It was so obvious that I wasn't going to get a word out that I didn't even try.

I walked sheepishly over to the couch and sank down, dropping my backpack onto the floor. I wished I could be tiny enough to hide under one of the cushions. Mom was pacing back and forth across the rug.

"I got a call from Dorathea when I was at the hospital. She told me you were running away. So I tried calling and when you didn't answer, I panicked and came home. I called everyone—your dad, Drake's grandmother, the police. You can't imagine how upset everyone was." Her eyes were burning with anger. They were like lightbulbs or branding irons. She might have given me a sunburn just by looking at me.

I didn't say anything.

"Celia." Her voice fell out of her mouth like a rock. "Was it just because you thought I was going on a date?"

I shrugged. "No."

"Not good enough," she said. "No shrugging, no *whatevers* or *I don't knows*. I'm sure the separation is difficult for you, and I've been trying really hard since your father left to be understanding and nonintrusive, but I don't know what to do anymore. Do you hate living with me so much?" She collapsed into the armchair and put her hands over her eyes. "Is that it? Say something," she demanded.

It made me ache to see my mom this upset, but I couldn't bring myself to console her. "I said a lot of things. I begged you to let me move to Atlanta. I begged Dad to stay. It doesn't matter when I say anything. You don't listen."

"I thought you would learn to be happy here with me." She slapped her hands on her thighs. "You're not even trying."

"I hate it here," I said, matching her intensity. "They're so mean to me at school. Did you even notice that I didn't have any friends before Drake? It's not like I just chose Dad. I needed to get out of Hershey, and you trapped me here." I was acutely aware of that crack inside of me.

My mom sat up straighter in her chair. "Kids are mean to you at school?"

That's when the tide came in. I opened my mouth to speak, but instead I started crying.

The Latin word for tears is *lacrimae*, which I learned in a book called *Human Tides: Our Waterways Within*. Tears are regulated by the lacrimal glands and are collected inside our bodies in a place called the lacrimal lake. The dam on the lake burst inside of me and flooded the floor in the living room. I was in deep, heaving sobs that barely let me catch my breath. All of the hurt from Sandy and the Book, from Dad leaving, it was so present it might have happened minutes ago instead of months. My mom came over to the couch and put her arms around me. She started crying, too.

After a few minutes, Mom stood up and got us a box of tissues from the coffee table, then brushed the hair back away from my face.

"Are you going to get back together with Dad?" I asked her, wiping my nose with a tissue.

She looked in my eyes for a long minute and then sniffled. "I don't think so, June Bug."

My heart balled up, a messy bunch of yarn. I thought about my dad in Atlanta, staying there.

"You should go get some sleep," she said. "No point in trying to go to school today."

I picked up my backpack and started down the hall to my room.

"It wasn't a date, you know," she called after me. "Simon is the first friend I've made on my own."

I could relate to needing a friend.

It was close to nine o'clock when I made it to my bed. Hershey High School was in session, as if nothing more important than second period was happening in the world. I fell onto my pillow without taking off my clothes. I slept. I did not dream.

It's a strange feeling waking up in the dark. For a moment, you have no idea what the world is up to. The sun might be obscured by nuclear fallout from a bomb that detonated while you were sleeping, or it might just be nighttime. The glowing letters on my alarm clock said 7:34 p.m., like it would on any normal Friday evening in September.

I wasn't ready to face my mom again so I lay there in the dark for a while, wondering what would happen next. Would my dad just stay in Atlanta, and we would always live here? Would Drake go back to New York with his parents? What would happen when I went back to school? What if having Drake as a friend was just a glorious, monthlong break from my otherwise lonely, outcast life?

Eventually, I pulled myself out of bed and emerged from my room. My mom was in the kitchen pulling a handmade pizza out of the oven and putting it on the cutting board to cool. My favorite dinner.

"I was just about to call you," she said, noticing me in the kitchen doorway.

I saw that the kitchen table was set with plates and forks; all the bills had been cleared away. I realized how long it had been since we sat down to dinner together at that table. It looked lonely with two plates sitting there instead of three.

"Thanks, Mom," I said, feeling like the tears might come back.

"I talked to your dad while you were sleeping," she said. "He didn't want me to wake you up and said you can email him back tomorrow. We decided that you are grounded for two weeks. You can only use your computer for schoolwork or to email family, and that's on the honor system. Your dad is going to visit Hershey next weekend so we can all talk about what's next, including where you want to live."

"Okay," I said, trying not to sound Dark. Dad was coming next weekend. That was supposed to be Drake's last weekend in Hershey, the weekend of Homecoming. There was a time when all I wanted was to have a say in where I would live. But I didn't care that much if I lived in Hershey or Atlanta if Drake wouldn't be in either place.

"And I talked to your principal. He told me about your poem getting hung up all over school and about what it said. Is that the reason you and Drake tried to run off to New York?"

I felt the tears coming back again. "Mom, I told the whole school that he's gay." I wiped away the first two drops from my cheeks, but more followed. "I promised him that I would never tell anyone."

"Oh, honey. You didn't do that. The person who posted your poem did." My mom drew me into a hug. "I wish you had told me what was going on. We're going to meet with Principal Foster on Monday morning and talk about everything. But for now, he said that you will have a two-day suspension for skipping school."

"Okay," I said into my mom's shoulder. It felt so good to be held by her.

That night my mom and I ate dinner and talked. We didn't talk about school or Drake or me trying to run off to New York in the middle of the night. She didn't bring up the suspension again. We talked about books that we liked and movies we wanted to see. She told me stories about the hospital, other nurses, and things patients had done.

After dinner, I helped with the dishes. We were clearing the last of them when my mom suddenly slapped her forehead and said, "Oh, I forgot." Then she went to the front door and picked up a paper grocery bag. "Someone left this for you," she said. "I found it on the porch while you were sleeping."

"Thanks." I nervously took the bag from my mom and then retreated to my room. I closed the door and sat down on my bed to open the sack. Inside was my black-and-white poetry journal that Sandy had stolen. Along with it was a letter.

Weird—

Got your book out of Sandy's locker. Don't ask how.

Suspension is just another word for freedom.

Clock

How did Clock know I was suspended? A tingly sensation rippled from my fingers down to my toes and a jolt of relief passed through me. I gave my poetry notebook a squeeze like it was a friend I hadn't seen in ages.

Then I got up and went to my desk and opened the bottom right-hand drawer. Under all the other papers and knickknacks, floaty pens, Hershey erasers and golf balls, I found it. *The Book.* It seemed smaller and lighter than I remembered. I turned on a lamp and opened the cover. There was the note titled, *Things Celia Needs to Change.* Even though a voice in my head told me not to, I started reading through the list. Grooming, clothes, friends, attitude. I read the suggestions saying I should brush my hair, shop at better stores, get some friends. I waited for the old black hole to form in my chest and for the pit in my stomach to grow into a tree and suffocate me with its roots and limbs. I waited for my throat to tighten and for my head to get light and my tongue heavy.

But something else happened.

As I read the list this time, I didn't feel sick. I didn't want to cry or disappear. Actually, I didn't feel much at all. The dull ache of disgust never started aching. I almost missed it. I realized that I didn't care about the Book the way I used to or what those ridiculous girls thought about me. The kids in Hershey probably weren't cool enough to get me. I didn't care if the whole school or even the whole world made me an outcast. All I cared about was Drake, and the fact that he might be leaving.

Tossing the notebook down, I lay back on my bed and pictured myself back in the bathroom, filling up the tub with water and bubble bath, finding my mom's razor blade. Had I really wanted to die that day? If I had died, I never would have met Drake. I never would have written a poem. Maybe there were more good things coming for me after this, and I just didn't know what they were yet.

Something had changed since that day. There was a strong place deep inside me, like I was a planet with an iron core. I could feel it in there, molten and churning. I wrapped my arms tightly around my pillow and fell asleep.

CHAPTER

34

The next day was Saturday, and September was drawing to an end. Leaves built themselves into piles against the mailboxes and the sides of houses. Pumpkins magically appeared on both of my neighbors' steps. Fall had fully taken root in Hershey, Pennsylvania.

Mom had to work but left me a chore list that said:

1. Laundry
2. Put a lasagna in the oven at four
3. Email your father!

I started by emailing Dad.

Re: I'm sorry

From: Celia (celia@celiathedark.com)

Sent: Sat 9/25 9:27 AM

To: James Door (jdoor@cocacolacompany.com)

hi, dad,

i'm sorry about leaving and not telling anyone where I was

going and making everyone worry. things have been hard
at school and some stuff happened that I want to tell you
about. can we talk about it when you come home next
weekend?
celia

I had an email from Dorathea waiting in my inbox.

Re: safe
From: Dorathea Eberhardt (deberhardt@berkeley.edu)
Sent: Fri 9/24 8:45 AM
To: Celia (celia@celiathedark.com)

celia,
i felt conflicted when i got your email. i believe in keeping
secrets, but it's dangerous to be fourteen and out on your
own. so i burned sage and chanted until i knew what to
do. after two hours in meditation, i started experiencing
visions. i saw you, ringed in a fog of smoke, boarding an
airplane.

at first the airplane was having a hard time taking off,
so the flight attendants opened the windows and started
tossing chocolate bars overboard until the plane was light
enough to fly. as the plane climbed higher in altitude, i
saw your spirit get lighter. finally, the plane was dancing
through a sky that did not contain clouds.

it was a really positive vision, but i still realized that i had to call your mom. she called me two hours later and said you were safe. i also saw your spirit animal, but i think it is wrong to reveal another person's spirit animal to her until she has the vision herself.

   don't run away again. never forget that you are special.

d

Dorathea had outdone herself on the weird emails. But who was I to judge? I had done a lot of weird things in the past month. Maybe my spirit panther got into some catnip.

I had another email in my inbox as well.

Re: Submission for Hershey High Lit Journal
From: Tara Flowers (editor@hersheyliterary.org)
Sent: Fri 9/24 9:21 AM
To: Celia (celia@celiathedark.com)

Dear Celia,
Our editorial team at the Hershey High Literary Magazine, *Nexus*, liked the poem you submitted: "whales are not fishes but mammals." We also saw your poem starting "Since Drake told me that day in the wooded lot," posted in the hall. We thought it was fabulous! We are inviting you to submit three to five poems to our next edition, published in late October. The theme is *Bitter Sweet*.

We also host a creative writing circle every Thursday after school in Mr. Pearson's classroom. Come write with us! We would love to see you there.

Sincerely,

Tara & Warren

Nexus Editors

I was light-headed. An editorial team saw my poem posted in the hall and they *liked* it! They were inviting me to a writing circle! I had no idea who Tara and Warren were. Were they like Drake and me? Was it possible we weren't really alone?

I was considering this radical possibility when the phone rang in the kitchen. It was Drake. Our conversation went like this:

Drake: "Any way you can get out of the house?"

Me: "I'm grounded for two weeks."

Drake: "I leave for New York tomorrow."

My heart ran away with the spoon. Tomorrow? Tomorrow! "Five minutes," I said.

"Wooded lot."

When I got close to Drake's house, I left the sidewalk and took my usual path through the neighbor's yard, behind the fence. I wasn't sure if his parents and grandmother were home, and I didn't want to be spotted in case they would report back to Mom that I was already breaking the rules of my grounding. Ducking behind the fence all the way to the wooded lot, I caught sight of Drake emerging from his lawn, zipping up his jacket. We met just beyond the tree line.

Before I could say a word, his arms were around me. He pulled me into a hug so tight that I lost most of my breath.

"Drumph," I said into his jacket.

"Huh?" He let a little space between us.

"Drake," I repeated with more enunciation. "I can't breathe."

"Oh, sorry." He released his arms from my ribs and let my lungs fill up again.

"Let's get farther away from the house." He took my hand and led me deeper into the trees. A few wild crocuses still poked their brave heads through the grassier areas of the lot, but overall it felt like a room that warm weather had been inhabiting and, one day, just up and left. We went to our usual log.

Drake sat down and shifted around to face me. "I told my parents everything after we dropped you off yesterday. We didn't even go to Gran's, we just sat in the car in a parking lot and talked. I told them about Japhy and the fight and your poem getting posted. I even showed them *Dream It! Do It!*"

"What did they say?" I asked, even though I really wanted to know about Drake leaving.

"My dad said that you can work hard and accomplish your dreams in life, and it does help to think positively and plan, but you can't force someone else to love you. He said that Japhy might be gay or he might not be, but that it was up to him to decide when and how he wants to tell people if he is."

"Do you believe him?" I asked.

"Yeah, I do. I guess I always knew it deep down. But Buddy's book made me feel better. It made me feel like I could have some control over coming out, over liking Japhy. *Dream It! Do It!* looked so ridiculous sitting on the dashboard between them," he added.

Drake seemed less glamorous to me now, sitting out there beneath the trees. He looked like a normal, sad, fourteen-year-old boy. The bruise under his eye was slightly lighter than the day before, the way a tan fades at the end of summer.

"They were really mad about what happened at school, with your poem getting posted and the fight. As soon as we finished talking, they drove to the school to talk to Principal Foster. They let me go home and sleep."

"Did they withdraw you? Is that why you're going back to New York?"

"No. Principal Foster found out about your poem before my parents got there, and they said he was really worked up about it, too. He said that the administration is going to fully investigate what happened, and they are taking it very seriously. They are giving it the weight of a hate crime. I've still got a three-day suspension for fighting because I threw the first punch, but he assured my parents that Hershey High School would be a safe environment for me after this."

"*After this?* But you're going back to New York. . . ." I said.

"My parents checked with both of the arts schools, that's the other reason they wanted to talk to Principal Foster. I'm still on the waiting list, but nothing is opening up. My mom said it's time to accept the fact that I'm not going to get into either one of them and make a decision. They came here this weekend to talk to me and Gran and the school about the possibility that I would stay in Hershey for the rest of ninth grade."

"But on the phone you said—"

"I'm going back to New York tomorrow so I can pick up some more of my stuff to bring back, I just wanted to see you before I left for three days. I decided I'm going to stay."

My heart sprouted wings and did figure eights through the treetops. It flew in loops and barnstormed the nurse log. Drake was staying! All year!

"I don't want to go to the school I'm zoned for in New York, and since I'm already out of the closet here, at least

I don't have to deal with telling people." He scowled at me, but playfully. "It's just for the year though," he added quickly. "I still want to go to art school as a sophomore."

My heart kept gliding around our heads.

"Are you going to be okay going back to school after what happened?" I asked.

"There is a whole chapter in one of my LGBT books about what to do if you get outed by someone else. It said that some queer people feel like it's a nightmare when they get outed, but some just feel relieved. Part of me feels relieved. Mom and Dad are helping me plan some strategies for handling things, and Principal Foster said the school would help, too. They're proud of me for going back."

A crow called from several branches above us. Drake looked up into the tree.

"So, the school called posting the poem a hate crime? Do they know Sandy and Mandy are responsible?"

"My parents told Principal Foster about Sandy, but they didn't have any proof. I don't know what's going to happen."

This was nothing like the revenge I imagined.

Drake's grandmother called his name from her back porch.

"Coming, Gran."

We walked hand-in-hand back through the wooded lot, having made it through one month of our ninth grade year. The future was a wide-open landscape and we were hiking without a map or compass. It was difficult to let go of Drake's hand when we got to the edge of the trees.

After one hug behind a wide oak, Drake walked out from under the canopy and back onto the grass of his grandmother's house. I turned and cut through his neighbor's lawn, behind the fence, and back into the streets of Hershey.

CHAPTER

35

It's Wednesday morning, and I'm waiting for Drake at our usual spot by the swing sets in the neighborhood. It's time to leave the quiet weightlessness of suspension and fall back into the noisy, gravity-filled atmosphere of high school. My only hope is that we don't burn up on reentry.

I haven't seen him since our secret meeting in the woods, but I know he will be here. I trust it.

I'm wearing my black hoodie, a black skirt, and my black boots with black tights. I guess I'm still dressed for battle, but, I don't feel Dark. I feel impossibly light, like I might float out of my shoes and over the school, drifting around in the breeze.

After school today, I will not go to the wooded lot with Drake. I will go the principal's office where I will meet with my Mom, Mandy and her parents, and Sandy and her parents. Hershey High asked for the meeting after my mom and I met with Principal Foster on Monday and I told him the whole story, from eighth grade up to last week. I showed him the Book that Sandy and Mandy made about me in middle school, but I also admitted to stealing Mandy's phone and writing things about Sandy on the bathroom walls. Hershey High takes bullying seriously; it looks like we might all have some dues to pay. Still, telling my story was like opening a door to a poorly lit room and letting the sun reach every corner.

I submitted five poems to the Hershey High lit magazine, and I'm planning to attend the after-school writing group on Thursday. During my suspension, my teachers emailed my homework assignments so I could keep up with the class. Mr. Pearson finally gave us a creative-writing assignment. The subject was Milton S. Hershey, founder of Hershey, Pennsylvania. I wrote mine in the form of a poem.

HERSHEY

Rolling out chocolate on marble
requires a thermometer filled with mercury.
Cocoa butter can ruin an entire batch.

Mercury is dangerous. One dropped thermometer
and the shop is contaminated. Mercury gets
in your cells and doesn't get out again, a toxic
river running under your skin.

Making chocolate is dangerous. It is also
delicious, rich and sweet to be the one
to clean the spatula and dip one secret
finger into the bowl.

ACKNOWLEDGMENTS

Writing your first novel is nearly impossible without support. I would like to sincerely thank my brilliant agent Dan Lazar, without whom this book might have included a treasure map. Joy Peskin's editorial compass was instrumental in keeping this book on course, and the staff at Viking Children's Books make a superb ship's crew.

My thanks to Richard Hugo House, Hedgebrook Writer's Retreat, Cooper Artist Housing, and Write Bloody Publishing for the kind of encouragement that makes artistic invention possible. Thank you to the national and international community of spoken word artists who coaxed my voice out of hiding.

The love of Louis and Judith Finneyfrock and the rest of my family has made everything in my life bloom.

Thank you, Joe Paul Slaby, for your nose for plot. Thank you to my friends, especially the ones who helped me get through high school. And thanks to Warren Austin Leyh. Every Celia needs a Drake.